The Secrets of
Grindlewood

THE QUEEN'S QUEST

Dedication

For Angelo

The Secrets of

Grindlewood

THE QUEEN'S QUEST

JACKIE BURKE

First published by Lindon Books in 2015,
9 Raheen Park, Bray, Co. Wicklow.
Web: www.grindlewood.com
Email: jackieburke@grindlewood.com

Paperback   ISBN: 978 1 909483 90 3
eBook – mobi format ISBN: 978 1 909483 91 0
eBook – ePub format ISBN: 978 1 909483 92 7
CreateSpace edition   ISBN: 978 1 909483 93 4

Produced by Kazoo Independent Publishing Services
222 Beech Park, Lucan, Co. Dublin
www.kazoopublishing.com

Kazoo Independent Publishing Services is not the publisher of this work. All rights and responsibilities pertaining to this work remain with Lindon Books.

Kazoo offers independent authors a full range of publishing services.
For further details visit www.kazoopublishing.com

Cover design by Andrew Brown
Cover and internal illustrations © Fintan Taite 2015
Printed in the EU

About the Author

Jackie grew up with her sister and three brothers in South Dublin. An avid reader and writer since her school days, she only recently began writing children's stories, having dreamed of doing so for quite some time. *The Queen's Quest* is the third book in the hugely popular Secrets of Grindlewood series.

Grindlewood is inspired by all that Jackie loves in nature – gardens, forests, wildlife – cats and dogs, and of course magic! Reading, hill walking and baking are just a few of her many hobbies. Jackie divides her time between writing and giving creative writing workshops to children and adults in schools and libraries around the country. She lives with her husband in Bray, County Wicklow. They share their home with a big fluffy cat called Millie.

Other books in The Secrets of Grindlewood series

The Secrets of Grindlewood (Book 1)

The Secret Scroll (Book 2)

'A classic tale to delight readers aged 8–12'
— Sue Leonard, author and journalist

Contents

Chapter One

THE QUEEN'S TORMENT

The Queen of the Wandeleis was deeply upset. Her mournful cries echoed through the tunnels and chambers of Hollow Hill, the underground home she shared with what remained of her magical clan.

The once-powerful and peace-loving queen had been cursed by her arch-enemies, the Worfagons, for refusing to give in to the warlocks' demands and reveal the Wandeleis' secret source of power. The tree curse was a fate worse than death, and so far all attempts to release the queen had failed. Hollow Hill was hurriedly built by the queen's loyal subjects to hide her grossly disfigured form. It quickly became a busy underground world for this gentle, war-weary people.

The queen swayed from side to side lamenting her fate, her long branches sweeping around her. Her arms had turned into branches that scraped along the ground as she stooped low. Her hands, now many leaves, brushed against the mound of earth built in a great arch above her.

Her body and legs had turned into a tree trunk. Her feet were replaced by roots that reached deep into the ground and stretched for half a mile in every direction. Around her sad and tormented face, her hair had become a wiry, matted bush and her voice was little more than a hoarse rasp.

'When will this torture end?' she cried. 'My reign is almost over and I am still stuck as a tree. How shameful!'

Her devoted subjects tried in vain to comfort her. A more recent companion was a small grey squirrel called Ripley. No one knew where he had come from, but he would amuse the queen sometimes, stroking her fuzzy hair or running up and down her branches. Mostly, he would just nibble away on nuts while the queen wailed.

Three senior professors gathered to talk. Pendrick, Flint and Sparks had spent years trying to free the queen, but their magic wasn't strong enough. They badly needed help.

'If we can't find our *Book of Magic* soon, I just don't know what we'll do,' said Sparks.

'We have utterly failed,' moaned Flint.

'We have done our best,' said Pendrick, 'but Sparks is right. Not only do we need the spells contained within the book to help us free the queen, but we desperately need to renew our powers – and we can't do that without the book either.'

'And we have another problem,' said Sparks. 'The Appointing Day is almost upon us. In less than two weeks, on October 31, the queen must announce her successor.'

'Goodness gracious! That's only twelve days away!' cried Flint.

Pendrick nodded. 'Queen Lyra has been our ruler for fifty years, the maximum time allowed. Wanda was her first choice to succeed her,' he said, 'but sadly that cannot be. She was such a gifted young witch and would have made a wonderful new queen.'

'It's difficult to know who else might be suitable,' said Flint. 'So many witches left us to make a new life somewhere quieter and safer, away from all the warring and destruction.'

'Well, it is our job to persuade Her Majesty to

choose, and choose quickly,' said Pendrick.

'Easier said than done,' muttered Flint.

'I know,' said Pendrick. 'That awful curse has changed her. She can be very unpredictable.'

Flint and Sparks looked forlorn.

'Come along,' said Pendrick, 'there's no time left to waste.'

As the professors headed towards the queen's chamber, the queen's fairy-in-waiting, Lotus, ran towards them with an urgent message.

'Her Majesty wishes to see you, all of us, in fact, everyone, right away.'

The professors glanced at each other.

'Perhaps this is it,' said Sparks.

'Maybe she is going to announce her successor after all,' said Flint, looking decidedly hopeful.

All of the Wandeleis in Hollow Hill stopped what they were doing and hurried to the queen. The huge chamber fell silent as the gathered crowd waited for the queen to speak. She shook her branches and pulled her nest of hair back from her face with her crinkled leaf-hands. The professors eyed each other.

'The leader of our enemy was defeated because of the courage and cleverness of our dear sister, Wanda,' began the queen. 'Sadly, the quest cost her everything, but she left enough clues behind for a brave group of friends from Grindlewood to finish it. Wanda chose them because she trusted them, and now, so must we.'

The audience murmured as the queen tried to look as regal as she could. She straightened her branches and spread them wide. Some of them creaked under the strain and a few withered leaf-hands fell off. This was an important announcement, but it wasn't what anyone in the audience expected.

'I want to meet these brave children and their pets. I am going to ask them to find the WABOM and return it to us.'

The professors groaned.

'But Your Majesty,' said Sparks. 'It was Wanda's years of difficult work that really defeated the warlock, not the children and their pets.'

'I agree,' said a wizard at the back of the chamber. 'They could never have done it without her magic.'

'Isn't that what I already said?' said the queen crossly.

'I thought it was the enchanted animals and birds who defeated Worfeus and saved Grindlewood,' said a witch.

'That's right, it was, but it's too dangerous for *children* to seek the *Book of Magic*,' said another.

'We can't ask non-magical people for help,' cried another witch. 'It's not what we do!'

'Very soon we won't have any magic left,' shouted another. 'We have to do something!'

'Quiet, please!' said the queen. Everyone hushed. 'This may be our last chance to get the book back. Only it will allow us to renew our magic, which, as you already know, is fading fast. We also have a duty to respect the Ancients who passed their magic and traditions to us through the centuries. We must do everything possible to preserve our way of life, and I will not be the queen who fails to do so.'

After a few moments of silence, the arguments began again as many witches and wizards argued their points of view across the chamber.

'Enough!' cried the queen impatiently. 'I have made up my mind. Everyone return to your duties. Professors, Lotus, please remain.'

When the chamber was empty, Queen Lyra turned to Pendrick, Flint and Sparks. 'No more arguments, gentlemen. There is no one else we can trust. The children and their pets have already proven themselves.

They will not be tempted to steal the WABOM for themselves. They are honest and true.'

'Your Majesty,' said Pendrick as calmly as he could, 'it is written that if our book, the WABOM, was ever stolen from us, it must be *given* back to us. We cannot simply find it and take it. We must rely on friends or allies to return it *to* us. And we have tried our hardest to think of who would be willing, able and trustworthy enough to undertake such a quest – but children?'

'And it wasn't just the children who defeated the warlock,' said Flint. 'The animals, birds, even the insects and pond life were involved.'

'That's right,' said Sparks. 'Indeed, it was the big dog, Timber, who was the real leader. He bravely led the quest and faced many dangers with no concern for himself. He was determined to find the scroll, decipher the spell, defeat Worfeus and save Grindlewood.'

'Precisely,' said the queen.

The professors looked at each other. They had just made a good case for the queen's new plan.

'Gentlemen, this plan is the only one we've got, and as you all keep pointing out, we are running out of time.'

'But aren't we putting the children in danger?' asked Pendrick.

'Well, Pendrick, unless you three have another plan, we have no other choice,' said the queen. 'Well, do you have another plan?'

'No, Your Majesty,' said Pendrick reluctantly.

'Very well, I will tell the children and their pets of this quest and then you will instruct them on the details,' said the queen. 'Although we have barely a glimmer of magic left, we will use every last bit of it to assist them.'

'Yes, Your Majesty,' said Pendrick.

'You may not like it, Professors, but the children will be needed,' squeaked Ripley. 'The animals and birds cannot carry the WABOM, even *if* they manage to find it. And the augurers told us that they have seen each part of the book in a different place, so the children will be busy on this quest, very busy.' The squirrel tittered loudly. The three professors glared at him.

'Thank you, Ripley. I have already sent a message with my butterflies to Grindlewood garden,' said the queen. The professors tried to stifle more groans. It seemed that the quest was already in motion. 'I have also heard quite a lot about the children's dog, Timber,' the queen continued. 'Ripley told me.' A few more withered leaves dropped from the queen's branches, as the squirrel snuggled into her nest of hair. He crunched loudly on a fresh chestnut.

'Do the children still have the enchanted treasures?' asked Sparks, trying to ignore the meddlesome squirrel.

'I believe so,' replied the queen. 'I gave them to Wanda to assist whomever she chose to seek out the WABOM after she discovered where it was. The blue ring, the string of gemstones and the compass brooch each have magic that is needed for this quest. The children probably aren't aware of this, but we will explain it to them.'

'Even the wise snowy owl doesn't know the magic of your enchanted jewels, Lyra,' squeaked Ripley.

The professors winced. Ripley was the only one who ever called the queen by her first name. They thought it was disrespectful.

'Will the augurers be able to pinpoint the whereabouts of each of the four parts of the WABOM, Your Majesty?' asked Pendrick.

'Audmund said they are working on it day and night,' said the queen, 'but I do wonder what is taking them so long. They seem to disagree about everything.'

'They certainly do,' said Flint under his breath.

'Do the children know anything about the WABOM?' asked the queen.

'I don't know, Your Majesty,' said Pendrick, looking at his puzzled friends.

'The animals do,' said Ripley.

'What's that, my squirrel?' asked the queen.

'I heard the hedgehog telling the fox about it one day, and then the fox told the others,' said the squirrel. 'I doubt if they know how important it is, or all it can do.'

'Do *you* know what it can do, Ripley?' asked Sparks, who was about to lose his temper, but the queen interrupted.

'We will find out what the children know when I speak with them – and Timber,' said the queen. 'I'm looking forward to meeting that dog. He will lead the children and his garden friends on this new quest for me, just as he did the last time.'

The professors bowed and turned to leave.

'Return in one hour, gentlemen. I would like a little time to rest before I reopen the tunnels.'

'The tunnels, Your Majesty?' said Sparks.

'Yes, it will allow the children to come and go to Hollow Hill.'

'Yes, Your Majesty,' said Pendrick quickly, before Sparks could blurt out any objections.

The professors eyed each other anxiously and then left. They had much to discuss.

❧

The tunnels had not been used for a long time. They stretched out like a huge honeycomb under the whole of Grindlewood, creating quite a village underground. After repeated raids by the Worfagons, Queen Lyra shut down all access to Hillow Hill. Eventually, one or two openings were restored to allow the Wandeleis secret access to Grindlewood village and the surrounding area, should they need it.

The professors stood outside the queen's door exactly one hour later. Flint and Sparks were still flustered.

'Is this really such a good idea?' asked Flint.

'Does she realise the risk she's taking?' added Sparks.

'I think so,' said Pendrick. 'Anyway, I don't believe we can change her mind now.'

When they entered the chamber, the queen looked impatient.

'Good, you're here,' she said. 'If I weaken mid-chant, you must continue the spell. Understood?'

'Yes, Your Majesty,' replied all three.

'Very well. Let's begin.'

After a minute of deep concentration, the queen let out a rasping cry and began to chant. The wizards stood patiently as she called out the words of the ancient spell and flexed her extended tree roots throughout the maze of tunnels. Slowly each one widened out, pushing the earth back, packing the clay and stones into thick, solid walls and ceilings until all the tunnels were open. The queen was exhausted. Her branches flopped down by her trunk.

'Pendrick, send out the dwarfs to check the tunnels,' she said. 'The children will discover them soon and then they will come.'

The three professors bowed and hurried off to carry out her instructions.

Chapter Two

A MYSTERIOUS MESSAGE

The weather was awful. High winds and sheeting rain continued for days. The children stayed indoors reading their books and playing games, sometimes jumping with the occasional flash of lightning or bang of thunder. The cats were curled up on the sofa and the dogs were sitting on the floor, half dozing, half listening to the children's conversation.

'Wow, all that rain is pooling in the garden. Look!' cried Jamie, standing at the window.

'Maybe the well will fill up,' said Jemima. 'I don't understand why it's always dry.'

'I don't think so,' said their dad, joining them. 'Any rain that falls into the well is leaking out, probably into an underground stream.'

'I think it looks a bit lopsided,' said Jamie.

'So it is,' said Greg, looking over his son's shoulder. 'I'll take a look when the storm is over. Don't go near it until then.'

'Greg, they're here!' called Gloria from the front room. Their visitors had arrived and Greg hurried to the hall door. Jamie eyed Jemima. Both of them wanted to check out the well and maybe their friends Luke and Abigail would like to come over and see it too.

The queen's root-shaking had caused quite a stir both under and over ground. The combination of all that shifting earth and clay and days of heavy rain had caused a lot of disturbance. Potholes and sink holes appeared, much to neighbouring Farmer Finlay's annoyance. Strange holes appeared in Grindlewood garden too. A few trees were leaning at strange angles as the soggy ground gave way just enough to unbalance the trunks. Luke and Abigail arrived and the four children were looking out the window when they saw the well tilt further to one side.

'Look, the well is sinking!' cried Jamie.

'Here it goes, over, and o-o-over, aaand, stop,' said Luke. 'Oh, it must be wedged on something.'

'We should check it out,' said Jamie. 'I've always

wondered if there could be more treasure down there in another box, or even a chest.'

'I guess it's worth a look,' said Luke.

'But it's still pouring rain,' said Abigail.

'We could get a better look from inside the fairy house,' said Jemima.

The dogs perked up. They were eager for some activity after days of sitting around. Once the children had wrapped up warmly in their coats, hats, scarves and Wellington boots, they all headed out the back door to the garden. It was a mad, splashing dash to the fairy house.

'Hey! Your butterflies are still flying about,' said Luke. 'Do they ever hibernate?'

'They should,' said Jamie. 'All the bees have already gone.'

'They look just like the last three, so why haven't they told us any secrets like the others did?' asked Jemima.

The children piled into the fairy house, leaving the door open for the dogs to come and go. Timber trotted in and sat on the floor. After all the action and excitement of the last quest, he liked to know what the children were up to – all the time. It was his job to keep them safe, after all.

'Whew,' said Abigail. 'I hope the rain stops soon.'

'Let's look at the treasures first,' said Jamie. 'It'll be easier to check out the well when the rain stops.'

They sat around the square table and took out the little wooden box from under the floorboards. Jemima lifted the lid and they gazed down at the contents: a small gold key; a sparkling crystal key; a man's gold ring with a large blue stone; a dainty diamond tiara; a large garnet brooch and a string of coloured stones.

'I wonder who owned all this stuff,' said Luke.

'We might never have found it if Timber hadn't sniffed it out,' said Jamie. 'He just knew there was something at the bottom of the well.'

Jemima held up the crystal key. Even on a dull day, it looked bright and sparkly. She put it down on the table.

'It's so very magical,' said Abigail. 'It's mentioned a lot in *The Book of Enchantments*.'

'That little book has been useful,' said Jamie. Abigail smiled. Her granddad had given her the faded old book from a special collection he kept in his cellar. They looked again at the glowing crystal key. Every now and then, it gave a little jump on the table, just enough to move it a tiny bit.

'A jumping, glowing key. How weird is that?' said Luke.

'Ever since we found it, I've been trying to figure out what it opens,' said Jamie. 'Whatever else it can do, it's still a key. It has to open something.'

'We tried everything in the house,' said Jemima, 'but it didn't fit anything.'

'It might have dark magic inside it,' said Abigail. 'We should keep checking it to see if it changes colour, or glows brighter, or … or anything else. It might mean something is about to happen.'

The others looked at her. She had a way of saying things that sounded mysterious and spooky, and she was usually right.

They turned their attention to the other pieces of the treasure trove. Both of the girls liked to try on the tiara, but Jemima's thick, curly hair made it pinch a bit. It sat easily on Abigail's sleek, straight hair and this annoyed Jemima just a little. She decided to try it on again anyway.

'It's still too small for me,' she said. 'I don't think it will ever fit unless I cut all my hair off.'

'The tiara belongs to you. It doesn't have to fit you,' said Abigail kindly.

'Thanks,' said Jemima. 'It looks really nice on you.'

Abigail put it on. It fit comfortably but she took it off quickly. Somehow it made her feel a little uneasy.

Both the boys liked the blue ring. When they wore it, the little dot of gold in the centre of the blue stone turned into the shape of a cross.

'This is so cool!' said Luke, putting it on his middle finger. His fingers were long and thin and the ring spun around. It fit Jamie's middle finger better.

'I really like it,' said Jamie, taking it from Luke. 'The way the cross changes is weird, though.'

Luke picked up the garnet brooch. 'Those four stones on the outside make it look a bit like a compass, but then again ...'

'If it is a compass, it might lead to more treasure,' said Jamie.

'What about the string of stones?' asked Abigail. 'Could all those stones be real?'

'Maybe,' said Jemima, wrinkling her nose as she always did when she wasn't sure.

'This little key could be important,' said Luke, turning the gold key over and over in his hand.

'I'd love to know what it opens too,' said Jamie.

They were quiet for a moment, wondering about the treasures. They were soon shaken from their thoughts by loud barking. It was Dougal. Timber trotted out to see what was bothering him. Then Timber began barking, and he kept on barking. Jamie looked outside through the crooked little window and followed the direction of the dogs' noses. Both were pointing in the same direction.

'Hey, they're heading over here!' cried Jamie. He put the treasures away quickly and they all ran outside. Luckily the rain had eased off and they waited as the butterflies approached.

All the pets had spotted them too and they gathered close to the fairy house.

'Do you think they have another message for us?' asked Teddy.

'If they do, I hope it's good news,' said Timber, 'and it will be the first message from this trio.'

The butterflies danced around Timber's head then landed between his ears. No one but Timber could hear anything. He listened carefully then shook his ears as the butterflies rose up and flew over to the children. There was a message for them too. They landed on their hair, each one in turn.

We are Chloe, Calista and Celeste,
You have been chosen to complete a quest.
You will be summoned soon by the queen,
She will explain what it will mean!

'Did you hear that?' cried Jamie.

'They must be talking about the Forest Queen, the one cursed to grow like a tree,' said Jemima. 'You remember, we read about her in *The History of Magic* book.'

'That's right,' said Abigail. 'She was the only queen we read about. I wonder where she is.'

'But that must have happened ages ago,' said Jamie. 'She's probably dead by now.'

'Maybe,' said Abigail, 'but magical people live longer than normal people.' The others looked at her again. 'It's in one of Granddad's books,' she said.

'Right,' said Jamie.

'What did they mean by "summoned by the queen"?' asked Luke. 'That sounds a bit heavy.'

'It sounds really important,' said Jemima. 'What should we do?'

'I guess we wait to be summoned,' said Jamie.

Timber howled.

Chapter Three

INTO THE TUNNELS

As there wasn't much they could do about the butterflies' message just yet, everyone turned their attention to the well. The garden was quite a mess after the storm and the ground was sludgy and mucky.

'Be careful everyone,' said Timber. 'Watch out for potholes.'

'Yikes!' said Norville. 'I really should have stayed at home.'

'Nonsense,' said Eldric. 'It's just a lot of rain and mud and holes in the ground and strange rumblings and …' The fox looked at Timber, then back at the hedgehog. 'Did anyone else hear those noises earlier?'

'Yes,' said Ramona. 'All the rabbits in the warren were terrified. It sounded like an earthquake.'

'Hmm,' said Timber. 'I wonder what it was.'

'It was definitely coming from underground,' said Teddy.

'The thunder had me confused,' said Dougal.

'Oh, I hate storms,' said Cindy, shivering.

'Well, I think this one is nearly over,' said Oberon. The snowy owl landed on the lopsided well. 'There's a break in the clouds behind the forest, so this should be the end of it.'

The children slowly approached the well.

'Be careful. It's really squelchy here,' said Jamie.

They leaned forward trying to see what was holding the well at such an awkward angle. Suddenly Timber began barking loudly.

'Get back,' he barked to the others. The animals retreated quickly and the birds flew upwards, out of the way.

'Move away!' cried Jamie. 'Something's wrong. Timber, come here, boy!'

Everyone backed away. With a sludgy groan and a heavy thud, a huge lump of earth slid away, revealing a deep hole beside the well. It was about three feet wide at the top and looked to be at least eight feet deep. A large chunk of granite was wedged under the well, preventing it from sinking further.

'Look at that!' cried Luke.

'The hole doesn't stop at the bottom,' said Jamie, peering down. 'It opens out. Wow! It looks like a tunnel. I wonder if it leads anywhere.'

'It looks like it was dug out on purpose,' said Luke.

'We *have* to take a proper look!' said Jamie.

'It's too far to jump,' said Abigail.

'We'd have trouble climbing out too,' said Jemima.

'Hang on, I'll get a ladder,' said Jamie. 'Don't go down without me!' Jamie raced off to the work shed. Luke ran after him.

They returned a few minutes later carrying a small wooden ladder. The boys dropped it into the hole, but the ladder was not as long as the drop. It was still an awkward slide from where they stood in the garden to the top of the ladder. They were going to get very mucky.

'Hey, look!' said Jemima, pointing.

'What now?' asked Jamie.

'The butterflies,' said Abigail.

'Again?' said Luke.

The three enchanted butterflies fluttered around the children's faces before flying down the hole.

'That's odd,' said Jamie. 'Why would they want to

go down there? It's dark and mucky.'

'We should follow them, shouldn't we?' said Jemima.

'I think so,' said Abigail. 'Look, they keep coming up and going back down again.'

'We trust them, don't we?' asked Luke. They looked at each other.

'Of course we do,' said Jemima.

Jamie lowered himself carefully onto the ladder and climbed down.

'It seems OK. I'm not sinking,' he called up.

The others followed. Timber stood barking at the top of the tunnel. He didn't like the children going somewhere strange without him and he couldn't climb down the ladder. It was too awkward for such a big dog.

'Wait a minute,' said Jamie, as he climbed back up, covered in mud. He ran to the fairy house, picked up the wooden stool and ran back to the tunnel.

'Luke, grab this.'

Luke took the stool and put it beside the bottom of the ladder.

'Timber, come on, you're coming with us,' said Jamie.

Timber barked and scraped the ground with his paws – that usually meant danger.

'I know, I know, it might be a little risky,' said Jamie, but Timber kept barking. 'Timber, I want you to come too,' said Jamie. 'We have to find out where this tunnel goes.'

Timber reduced his barking to a growl and walked over to the hole. He peered down, sniffing the air. Jamie stood at the top of the hole and held his dog.

'Timber, I'll lift you down. Then you have to jump onto the stool and then to the ground, OK?' Timber looked at Jamie as if to say, 'You're kidding, right?' But Jamie was determined. 'We're going anyway, Timber,' said Jamie, as he climbed down the ladder again.

Timber knew that Jamie was tricking him, but he was also a bit curious. He glanced back at his garden friends, shook his ears and prepared to scramble down.

'See you later, then,' called Teddy.

The animals and birds watched as Timber prepared to leap into the hole. Luke stood on the ladder with Jamie. Timber jumped down, bounced awkwardly off the two boys, landed on the stool and then tumbled onto the tunnel floor.

'Good boy, Timber, good boy,' said Jamie, climbing down. 'Now we're ready to go.'

It was dark in the tunnels. At first there was a shaft of light coming down the hole, but it faded as they moved further in. Jamie took a torch from his coat pocket and switched it on. They stood still and looked ahead. The tunnel seemed to go on and on. They walked slowly and carefully, watching their step, looking from side to side, wondering if it would collapse, what might appear, and where it would lead. Timber trotted bravely in front.

'What is this place?' asked Jamie.

'I wonder how long it's been here,' said Luke.

'It must be true,' said Abigail, looking at Jemima.

'What must?' asked Jamie.

'Abigail and I read about tunnels in one of *The History of Magic* books,' said Jemima.

'Really?' said Jamie.

'Really,' said Abigail. 'In volume six it said that they were built by goblins and dwarfs.'

'What?' cried Jamie.

'Uh oh,' said Luke.

'That's what it said,' said Jemima.

'They were looking for gold,' said Abigail. 'The

dwarfs did most of the tunneling and the goblins made things with the gold they dug up.'

Jamie turned around to stare at the girls.

'Seriously?'

Abigail and Jemima nodded.

'Nothing would surprise me any more,' said Luke. 'Not after meeting a real witch, seeing a real warlock, being hit by two spells, stuck in a statue, seeing enchanted butterflies and …'

'Yes, yes, we know,' said Jamie. 'But goblins and dwarfs mining for gold – here?'

'Jamie, shine the torch on the walls over there. Look!' said Jemima.

They stopped. Specks, streaks and lumps of deep yellow were dotted around the walls and ceiling of the tunnel.

'Is that, really, is it …?' said Jamie.

'Gold?' finished Luke.

'It must be,' whispered Abigail.

'Then this *must* be a goblin tunnel,' said Jemima, delighted.

'And, where are the goblins now?' asked Jamie.

'Good question,' said Luke. 'They might not like to find us here.'

'There's a lot more gold up ahead,' said Jamie. 'I don't think we need the torch any more.'

'So much gold,' said Jemima, as she reached out to touch the walls. 'This tunnel must lead somewhere very exciting.'

'Or very important,' said Abigail.

'Any ideas what we'll find at the end?' asked Luke.

No one answered. They really didn't know.

Chapter Four

THE BUZZARD AND THE EAGLE

Oberon Owl was unsettled. He had flown into the garden, hoping to have a chat with Timber, but now Timber had gone down the tunnel with the children.

'Oh dear, I really wanted to talk to him,' said the owl.

'What's the matter, Oberon?' asked Teddy. 'Is there anything I can do?'

'Oh, hello, Teddy. Not really. I mean, well, perhaps,' muttered the owl.

Teddy felt a little put out, but he waited patiently for the owl to explain.

'Well, Teddy, I've been wondering what Bodric Buzzard is up to,' said the owl, raising his eyebrows, 'and also what Gildevard is doing.' Before Teddy could say anything, Oberon chattered on. 'And there are a few other things that don't add up. For instance, why did Bodric order his hawks to kill Bryony Barn Owl last summer? And why wouldn't Gildevard allow me to listen in on his conversation with the buzzard, or tell me what had been said once we returned from Bodric's camp?'

'Oh,' said Teddy, 'I see.'

Dougal and Eldric joined them.

'As for Bodric,' said Eldric, 'we know he has a habit of doing favours for unsavoury characters like Worfeus in return for getting something he wants.'

'Yes,' said Teddy. 'Whatever he's doing, it's probably bad news.'

'And what about Gildevard?' said Oberon, fluffing his eybrows again. 'Does he ever tell anyone what he's really up to?'

'No, he doesn't,' said Teddy. 'Eagles are loners and don't usually confide in anyone. That's why Timber is a little worried about Gildevard's acquaintance with Bodric. It could turn nasty.'

'Agreed,' said Oberon. 'I must admit I have admired the golden eagle for a long time. He is a very clever bird and so dedicated to knowledge and learning. He is well respected by professors of history and magic everywhere. Perhaps we should be more concerned about Bodric.'

'Well, we certainly know how crafty and wicked that buzzard is,' said Dougal.

'Timber knows something is bothering you, Oberon, and he thinks you're cooking up a plan,' said Teddy. 'Is he right?'

'Yes, I do have an idea,' said the owl before chuckling a little. He always found it amusing when Timber knew what he was thinking. 'I want to fly north to Bodric's camp and spy on him. I was hoping to take the sparrows with me, as lookouts.'

'I see,' said Teddy.

'It's one way of finding out what Bodric's up to,' said Dougal.

'OK,' said Teddy, 'but be careful. The sparrows are very brave but they're no match for Bodric and his gang.'

'Understood,' said the owl. 'Let Timber know where we've gone when he returns.'

He flew off to talk to the sparrows. They were always keen for adventure, ever since Wanda had enchanted them with *stunning* beaks. The blackbirds were close by and overheard the conversation.

'Can we come too?' they chirped.

'This could be very dangerous,' said Oberon. 'You know what happened the last time we went to visit Bodric – Bryony Barn Owl didn't return.'

'We haven't forgotten,' said Binky. 'We just thought you might need a few more birds to keep lookout.'

Oberon thought about it for a moment, muttering to himself and burrowing his beak in his feathers. 'It's a long flight and the weather can be harsh. A few more scouts would be helpful, but I will be the only one to go close to the camp.'

'No problem,' said the four blackbirds together.

'All right then. We shall feed up tonight and head off just before dawn,' said Oberon. The owl tooted and flew off to hunt. The little birds went to catch some sleep.

The weather started out calm, but once they came within a few miles of Bodric's camp, the clouds gathered and the wind whipped up again, gusting unpredictably. The smaller birds were exhausted by the time they reached their destination: a bleak, barren scrub land. They landed at a safe distance from where

Bodric and his followers were gathered.

'We can't go any closer until dark,' said the owl. 'Try to get some rest and keep very quiet.'

The birds huddled together and took a short nap. Oberon remained alert, hoping he had done the right thing by bringing them along.

When it was finally dark enough to move closer to Bodric's camp, they flew in silent and low, ducking behind the bushes that grew here and there. Soon, they could hear squawking and cackling. Bodric and his army of hawks and buzzards seemed to have enjoyed quite a feast that evening. Hopefully they would be relaxed and lazy after a big feed.

'I'm going over to the scrubby patch beside that big boulder over there,' said Oberon. 'Sparky and Spindle, you watch from that clump of bushes on the left as we agreed – no closer. You four blackbirds split into pairs: two to the right and two to remain here. You know the warning call if you see or hear trouble. And watch out for those hawks!'

The smaller birds flew to their positions. They watched the snowy owl fly perilously close to the camp to try to see and hear as much as possible.

Bodric and his ragged army were gathered in a

tight bunch. Some of them were still plucking at a carcass. Others had fallen asleep, bloated with food. It wasn't long before the owl's sharp ears heard something interesting over all the chortling.

'This feast is as good as the one we had after Worfeus was finally sent packing,' spluttered Bodric, gobbling down another sliver of meat.

'What a clown!' said one buzzard. Other buzzards chuckled.

'A complete buffoon!' laughed Bodric. 'I only killed the barn owl to make that big-headed warlock think we had some kind of "partnership" going on. Ha ha!'

The buzzards laughed loudly. Oberon gulped. It sounded like he had been lucky to escape alive the last time he had been there.

'As for that pompous golden eagle,' said Bodric, 'he'll do anything for knowledge.' There were roars of approval from the buzzards. The hawks sniggered.

'The way you fooled him about that spell chant was hilarious!' said one.

'Yes,' said Bodric, 'but it's a pity those children figured it out. If they hadn't, the spell wouldn't have worked and Worfeus would have destroyed all of Grindlewood. Kaboom!' He ripped at another bone. 'Yes, shame. I'm certain a Worfagon wipe-out spell would have reduced Grindlewood to rubble and then we might have discovered the source of the Wandeleis' power. No one has ever found it, but I will. I'll find it for Zora, and it will make her unstoppable.'

'But where is it, Bodric, this ultimate source of power?' asked a buzzard.

'What? Never mind. No one knows, but I'm convinced it has something to do with that garden, and those silly do-gooders have been getting in the way.'

'Yes, those annoying children and their pets are quite the little army now, aren't they?' said a beady-eyed falcon with long yellow talons. 'They found something in that old book of theirs that spoiled your last plan for world domination.' Bodric glared at the smaller bird. 'Indeed,' continued the falcon, 'they were a lot more trouble than you expected.'

'Don't overstep your position, Festus,' said Bodric. 'You may be Zora's chief *messenger*, but you might outgrow your usefulness some day, so be careful.' Bodric lowered his ugly beak right into the falcon's face. Festus shuddered and retreated.

'Bodric, what are you going to do about that big dog?' said an old, buckled buzzard sitting near a pile of bones. 'He won't give up easily.'

'Do be quiet, Benny! Timber is not important,' said Bodric. 'Just forget about him. We have other things to think about, like preparing for Zora's return.'

'I think this dog is different,' said Benny. 'He's clever and brave, and loyal too.'

Bodric ignored him.

'When do you expect Zora to arrive, Bodric?' asked Festus.

'Soon, Festus, soon,' said Bodric. 'In the meantime, we need to find the rest of the WABOM. The Forest Queen is looking for it too, but we are several steps ahead of her. I have one part of it already – *The Book of Darkness* – ha ha!' The buzzards chortled their approval. 'I have instructed my allies to seek out the other three parts. If they fail, I will be sending you and the hawks to continue the search.'

'But Bodric –' began one hawk.

'Don't "*but Bodric*" me!' he roared. 'You know I don't like moaning. Our task is to find the four parts of the WABOM, so that is what we shall do.'

While his army chortled and scuffled about, Bodric continued his mutterings of greatness. 'Yes, once I get my hands on all four parts of the WABOM, everything will change. I will find the ultimate source of power, and Zora will have her revenge. She will reign supreme, and I will be rewarded handsomely for helping her.'

The old buzzard, Benny, looked over at him with eyes full of doubt. He shook his scrawny head and then shuffled away. There was no point in arguing with his violent cousin.

Behind the boulder and the scrub grass, Oberon was stunned. Bodric had plans all right, crazy plans by the sounds of it. He flew back to the safe spot and the other birds joined him.

'I knew he was up to something,' said Oberon. 'Come on, let's get out of here.'

Gildevard the golden eagle lived in a large, untidy nest on a cold and windy cliff top. He rarely had visitors but that didn't bother him. He liked solitude. His study was a sheltered hole on the side of the mountain. There he kept piles of books, papers, notes and artefacts — all the things that he had gathered, studied, learned and relearned over many years.

He shuffled about, scattering some of his papers. 'Where are those notes?' asked the eagle, crossly. The apprentice lifted a bunch of papers with his beak. 'No, not those, the notes I was working on during the summer.'

'Do you mean the notes you made from the secret scroll?' asked the kestrel.

Gildevard glared at him.

'Yes, that's right, Kelvin. Is there a problem?'

'No, sir,' replied the smaller bird of prey. 'I was just wondering if you intend telling your friends in Grindlewood that you spotted something else on the scroll, something important.'

'That doesn't concern you,' said the eagle. 'Now, I want you to copy all the notes I made in dark blue ink. Make two copies, in black ink this time, and make sure all the lines are in the right order. I still can't figure out whether it is a spell, a potion, a message, a secret code or … hmm, yes, perhaps a code of some sort.'

Kelvin sighed.

'Please try not to be so uninterested, Kelvin, this is a very exciting time for me,' said the eagle. 'I may be about to decipher something incredibly important, and I will soon have my first and perhaps my only chance to read *The Book of Wisdom*. I am sure I can figure out this code once I have seen the book.'

'Yes, sir,' said Kelvin as he started flicking through the notes and scraps of paper with blue talon-scrawl on them.

'Only very learned people can read and understand *The Book of Wisdom*, you know,' continued Gildevard. 'I am one of the few, outside of the most learned magicians, of course, who might actually be *able* to read it.'

'Yes, sir,' said Kelvin absentmindedly. He knew that the eagle was never going to get near *The Book of Wisdom*. There were others who had plans for that book, plans that Gildevard knew nothing of.

'Work hard at the copying, Kelvin,' said the eagle. 'I need to stretch my wings. I expect you to have made good progress by the time I get back.'

The eagle flew off and the kestrel got to work, although he had his own reason for doing so. He was going to make an *extra* copy of the notes – a copy for himself.

Gildevard had not told anyone in Grindlewood what he had seen on the secret scroll. 'Why should I?' he thought. 'They only needed me to translate the spell to defeat the warlock and I did it.' But Kelvin's words were troubling him. Keeping secrets about the scroll from the residents of Grindlewood was unfair, and on top of that, he was about to play a very dangerous game.

When Bodric and Gildevard had met in early summer, they had arranged to trade what Gildevard had seen on the scroll for information Bodric had on the whereabouts of *The Book of Wisdom*. The eagle had no real intention of telling the buzzard what was truly in the code. He would make up something and hope that the buzzard would believe him. It was a risk worth taking. After all, the chance of reading *The Book of Wisdom* had simply been too great to ignore, and so he had made a deal with the devious buzzard. Now, that deal was clouding the eagle's judgment.

The kestrel dipped his talons into the pot of shiny black ink. Gildevard had taught him to write in several ancient witch languages. Those lessons had been difficult but useful. 'That eagle is so clever yet so foolish,' he thought, stroking the words and symbols carefully. 'He's so busy dreaming of what he'll find in *The Book of Wisdom* that he can't see what's happening right under his own beak! Silly bird!'

Kelvin had plans for this secret code. It must be important if Wanda had written it on the scroll, and that meant it was valuable. Others would want it. Zora might even reward him for it. Anyway, it was time for a change. Being a double spy was exhausting. In future, Gildevard could do his own copying and researching. As for Bodric, he was just a ragged scavenger who had been lucky. 'Yes,' he thought, 'it's time for Kelvin Kestrel to make a name for himself. Things are going to change a lot around here.'

Chapter Five

HOLLOW HILL

The children and Timber stopped suddenly. The tunnel they had been following suddenly split in three. While they wondered what to do, Timber sniffed around and then barked.

'What is it, Timber?' asked Jamie. The dog barked again, pointing his nose at the butterflies. They were all heading in one direction – down the centre tunnel. It wasn't the most obvious choice as it was narrower and it sloped downwards, deeper underground. The children were nervous.

'Should we go on?' asked Luke.

'Timber seems to think so,' said Jamie.

'Both Timber and the butterflies want us to go down the middle one,' said Abigail. 'So, it must be the right one, mustn't it?'

'It has to be,' said Jemima.

'I wonder where the other two tunnels go,' said Luke.

'Timber wouldn't lead us into trouble, would you, Timber?' said Jamie. The dog wagged his tail.

The children walked on, though a little slower than before. Lumps of gold were glowing in all the walls and overhead, lighting the way with soft, yellow light. After a few minutes they saw another, narrower tunnel turn off to the left, and a bit further on another one turned to the right.

Eventually, the tunnel widened out into a circular chamber lit by huge candles attached to heavy brass rings on the walls. Colourful rugs were scattered about on the ground and wooden chairs stood in between other tunnel openings that led off to places unknown. Timber was picking up lots of interesting scents.

'Wow, this is amazing,' said Jamie.

'Someone must live down here,' said Luke.

'I think it's a lovely room,' said Jemima.

'It's called a chamber,' said Abigail. 'I saw a picture just like this in one of Granddad's books.'

'Hello and welcome!' said Pendrick.

The children whirled around. They saw a thin,

middle-aged man waiting to greet them. He wore a long, dark cape and shiny shoes with buckles. He had a narrow but kindly face and a neat grey beard. The professor smiled warmly at the children. Timber gave a little bark and trotted over to him. He wasn't at all bothered by this stranger. That was a good sign.

'Eh, hello,' said Jamie. 'Em, we're not sure where we are.'

'Or whether we should be here at all,' said Luke. 'Sorry for barging in.'

'Hello, my name's Jemima. This is my brother, Jamie, and my friends Abigail and Luke,' said Jemima, pointing to the others in turn.

'Yes, I know who you are. My name is Professor Clive Pendrick. You are in the reception chamber of Hollow Hill, home of the Forest Queen and her magical clan, the Wandeleis. Her Majesty is expecting you. Please, follow me.'

The children didn't move. Pendrick stopped and turned around.

'Didn't you get the message from the butterflies?' he asked.

'Eh, yes, I think so,' mumbled Jamie.

'Oh, the message,' whispered Jemima.

'Are we late?' asked Abigail.

'Not at all, perfect timing. Please, come this way,' said Pendrick.

The wizard led them down another, smaller tunnel and then they turned left down another one, where they stopped.

'Now we are in the queen's *outer* chamber,' said Pendrick. 'When we go into the *inner* chamber, you should address her as "Your Majesty", and please answer any questions truthfully. Now, wait here for a moment.'

Pendrick disappeared behind a heavy, wooden door with a huge iron ring for a handle. The children waited anxiously.

'Didn't the butterflies say something about a *quest* as well?' whispered Luke.

'Yes, they did,' said Jemima. 'This could be it!'

'You mean like what happened last summer?' said Jamie.

'This all seems a bit different,' said Abigail.

Professor Pendrick returned quickly.

'We will go in shortly,' he said. 'I should tell you that our queen has been dreadfully cursed. It happened a long time ago. Our enemies, the Worfagons, attacked and destroyed her palace, took her most prized possessions and cursed her to grow in the ground like a tree. It was a terrible, terrible day.'

The children stared at him, speechless, as the professor explained some more.

'We built this structure to hide the queen from the world, all worlds, as was her wish. Outside, it looks just like a gentle hill in the landscape. Underground, we built an entire village in amongst the goblins' tunnels. It is quite a community now.'

Pendrick paused, slightly embarrassed that his queen had to live in so unseemly a place, underground.

'Her Majesty has grown into quite a large tree and her height pushes the ground above ever higher. She is quite a frightful sight but I must ask you not to show too much surprise, if possible.' Pendrick looked at them to see if they understood. Each of the children nodded. 'Good,' he said. 'Her Majesty opened the tunnels especially to allow you in to Hollow Hill. This is a rare privilege for non-magical people.'

Still a little stunned, the children followed the wizard into the queen's chamber. Nothing Pendrick had said could have prepared them for what they saw.

After twenty-five years growing in the ground, the

Forest Queen was over fifteen feet tall and would have stood taller if she hadn't been so stooped under the mud and clay ceiling. Now, in late October, her leaves were falling, and many dry, withered leaf-hands lay scattered on the ground.

Her once beautiful face was lined and worn. Her large green eyes were full of frustration and shame, yet at the same time soft and sad. Her long, silky, black hair had been replaced with a mousy-grey, tangled bush that looked more like a nest for birds than a queen's beautifully groomed tresses. The children stared up at her.

'Welcome, children,' she said.

'Hello,' said Jamie. The others said nothing.

'Welcome to Hollow Hill, my home since I was cursed by the wretched Worfagons. I'm sure Pendrick has told you.' The children nodded. 'Good, now where is this brave dog, Timber?' asked the queen. Timber trotted out from behind Jamie and moved towards the queen. Jamie grabbed his dog by the collar. He didn't want him to go near this weird talking tree.

'Timber, sit, sit,' said Jamie, firmly. Timber obeyed.

'Come here, Timber,' said the queen.

Timber growled a little, unsure of what to do. He

looked at Jamie, then stood up and began to trot forward again. Jamie pulled him back.

'I want to see your dog,' said the queen a little louder.

'Let him go to the queen,' whispered Pendrick.

'What?' cried Jamie.

'Let him go,' urged Pendrick.

Jamie reluctantly gave in. Timber stopped in front of the tree trunk and sat down. The queen lowered her branches so that a few leaf-hands could reach him. She stroked Timber's head and ears. He sat quietly as the queen petted him.

'He is so like Tyrus,' she murmured. 'I never thought I would ever see a dog so like my beautiful Tyrus. Perhaps you are descended from him, Timber.'

Jamie glared at Pendrick, his eyes brimming with the question, 'Who was Tyrus?'

'Tyrus was Her Majesty's pet wolf,' Pendrick explained quietly. 'He was killed by the Worfagons while trying to protect her. The queen was distraught at losing her beloved pet.' The other wizards looked anxiously at each other.

'What does she want with Timber? He's *my* dog,' said Jamie in a loud whisper.

'Ahem, Your Majesty,' said Pendrick, 'you have something to say to the children.'

'Yes, I do,' said the queen. 'Last summer, you and your Grindlewood friends succeeded in defeating Worfeus after so many had failed. I congratulate you and I thank you. Now, I have another quest for you.'

'What?' cried Jamie.

'Another quest?' cried Luke. The girls took a sharp breath but didn't say anything. They were all excited by magic, but suddenly the idea of another quest was scary. They were about to protest, but the queen continued.

'Wanda was trying to locate my most prized possession, the WABOM, but she died protecting our secrets, before she could finish her quest. Now I need you to finish it for her.'

'We don't know anything about a WABOM,' said Jamie. 'We knew that Wanda wrote a scroll, but that was destroyed.'

'It was burnt to ashes,' said Luke.

'It wasn't our fault,' said Jemima. 'The birds tried to save it, but –'

'Oh yes, the owl and the eagle,' moaned Ripley. He didn't like birds of prey.

'Look at me!' cried the queen. 'I cannot stand this any longer. You must do this. You must! It is the only way I can be free of this curse and we can save our way of life.'

'What? How?' said Jamie. 'We're not wizards or witches.'

'Her Majesty has another idea,' said Flint gently.

'Jamie, isn't it? You are the brave one, like your dog,' said the queen, quietening a little.

Jamie felt a little chuffed at being called brave, but then he got a shock, just as the others did.

'Let me explain,' said the queen. 'WABOM stands for *The Wandeleis' Ancient Book of Magic*. It contains our oldest and most powerful magic. When it is returned, my professors will be able to consult that magic to create a spell to free me. Without it, I am doomed – we are all doomed. Magic of such power and complexity should not be used by anyone but the Wandeleis. Our enemies, should they find this book, will use it to destroy us. It must be returned before it is too late. You, children of Grindlewood and all your animal friends will – find – the – WABOM. It is my

~ 60 ~

command. It is now your quest.'

'But how can we do that without being stopped by our parents, and without knowing where to look for it or even what the book looks like?' asked Luke.

'Ah, Luke, the bright one,' said the queen. 'Wanda knew you were smart and that she could trust you, all of you – the animals, the birds, all the residents of Grindlewood. It is really Wanda who has chosen you for this quest, just as she chose you for the last. Who else can succeed if not those who are worthy?'

'We're *worthy*?' muttered Jamie.

'I think I read that in one of our books,' said Jemima.

'I'm sure you have, Jemima,' said the queen. 'You are a believer, one who truly believes that magic is everywhere. Surely this makes sense to you?'

'Well yes, but …'

'Well then,' said the queen, 'why do you protest?'

Jamie glared at his sister, who looked back at him apologetically.

'So where is this book and how are we supposed to get it?' asked Luke.

Jamie turned the other way and glared at Luke. Luke looked back at his friend. 'What choice do we have?' he asked quietly. 'She's a queen, a witch queen.'

'The WABOM is made up of four parts,' said the queen. 'Each part, or book, has its own name and purpose. As a whole, the WABOM has other, special qualities, but you need not concern yourselves with those now. It is extremely important that it is returned to us immediately.' The queen paused and looked at them closely. 'Have you by any chance come across a small gold key?'

The children glanced at each other. They knew this key.

'You do have it,' said the queen, watching them carefully. 'Was it with the other treasures – the brooch, the tiara, the string of stones and the ring?'

'Huh?' said Jamie. 'How did you know?'

'Yes,' said Jemima, before she could stop herself. 'They were all together.'

'Excellent!' said the queen. 'So Wanda did find it. Thank goodness! You must bring the key and the treasures to me and I will explain their magic. You will need some of them to help you on this quest.'

'How did you know we had the treasure?' asked Abigail suddenly. She had been very quiet until now.

'Ripley, my companion squirrel, told me,' said the

queen. 'He keeps me informed of what is going on overground.' The queen stroked the squirrel, who smiled coyly. 'Why didn't you tell me about the gold key, Ripley?'

'I, eh, never saw it, Lyra, never saw it,' said Ripley.

'Never mind, we know where it is now,' said the queen.

Timber growled. He had taken an instant dislike to the squirrel. There was something sneaky about him.

'You must begin the quest immediately,' said the queen abruptly.

'But what has it got to do with us?' asked Jamie, bluntly. 'Why can't your own people find it?'

'They should, but they can't,' replied the queen sharply. 'Let me explain a little more. The Wandeleis are an ancient magical people who have lived in these parts for centuries, long before any non-magical people came here. This is our land, our way of life, our magic. Anyone who lives in Grindlewood, as you do now, is expected to protect it from harm, just as we have always done. We have helped your kind in the past, so you are obliged to help us in return. You have proven yourselves to be *worthy,* so you do not have a choice.'

'If I may, Your Majesty,' said Pendrick. The queen nodded but she was clearly agitated. She started swaying while Ripley stroked her hair.

'You cannot refuse the Forest Queen,' said the wizard quietly, drawing the children a little back. 'We desperately need outside help, your help. We cannot trust anyone else, and we have very nearly run out of time – and magic.'

'Without the WABOM our magic will fail,' said Sparks. 'Every twenty-one years, at Halloween, the queen uses the WABOM to perform the Renewal Charm. This is how we renew our magical powers and that is why we cannot help her without the book.'

'We do not know how much longer our magic will last,' said Pendrick. 'The renewal of our magic is already overdue.'

'We have no one else we can turn to,' said Flint.

'But why did Wanda choose us? She didn't know us,' said Jamie.

'She knew me, and lots of the animals and birds in Grindlewood,' said Luke.

'Do you really want us to do this?' said Jamie crossly.

'Of course not. You heard what I said,' said Luke, turning to the professors. 'How can we do this,

Professors, even with magical treasures? I mean, what about our parents, school, everything. Where do we look for this book? How will we know it? We can't just disappear on a quest, like, like –'

'Like you did before?' finished Pendrick.

'Well, sort of,' said Luke.

'We can take care of that with some memory mist and a few other simple spells,' said Pendrick. 'We can still do *some* magic, but we need the WABOM to undo the dark magic of the tree curse.'

'We have a way of twisting time and space,' said Sparks with smile. 'I think you'll enjoy that.'

'We'll explain it to you later,' said Pendrick, seeing the children's confused expressions.

'I'm worried about Timber,' said Jamie. 'I don't like the way the queen looks at him. She had better not hurt him, or I'll, I'll …'

Jamie wasn't sure what he could do to a witch queen, but he was right to be worried. While the children were talking to the professors, they didn't see what was going on behind them. When Timber shook his head, his collar made a strange sound. The children turned around to look at him.

'What's that? What did you do to him?' cried

Jamie, examining his dog. He saw that Timber's leather collar had been replaced with a silver-studded one. It had strange engraving on it and it gleamed in the candlelight. The exchange had happened so quickly, even Timber didn't have time to react.

'Let me make it clear to you all,' said the queen. 'Unless you return the WABOM to me, your dog will not be returned to you.'

'NO!' cried Jamie. 'You can't take Timber from me!'

'I have placed Cordelia's Collar around his neck,' said the queen. 'Only a Wandelei queen can unlock its powerful charm. You cannot remove it and I will not remove it until you successfully complete the quest. If he does not return here every day, the collar will choke him.'

'Oh, Your Majesty,' gasped Flint.

Pendrick winced and frowned. Sparks had a coughing fit.

'No, you can't, not to Timber, NO!' roared Jamie. He was horrified and furious all at once. Jemima was about to cry. Abigail was trembling, her hands covering her mouth in case she screamed. Luke went very pale.

'Timber will not be harmed provided you stick to your side of the bargain,' said the queen.

'Bargain? What bargain?' cried Jamie. 'You're forcing us to do this and you're threatening Timber.'

'Jamie, we have to agree,' said Luke through gritted teeth.

'We'll do it, Jamie,' said Jemima.

'With the wizards' help and the enchanted treasures, we can do it,' said Abigail. 'We'll make sure Timber is freed.'

'Go home now,' said the queen. 'Timber must return with you every time you come here to report to me. Remember the magic of Cordelia's Collar. Remember too, if the WABOM falls into the wrong hands, terrible things will happen, not just here, but in all of Grindlewood. Go and return tomorrow with the jewels and the gold key.'

The queen folded her branches tightly to her trunk. Ripley sniggered, scrambled down the tree and ran off.

'What bargain?' said Jamie, over and over. He was so upset even though Timber seemed all right. He snuggled up to Jamie, his shiny new collar a clear reminder of what was at stake. Jamie picked up the old one off the floor and put it in his pocket. The children walked slowly out of the chamber. Professor Pendrick followed quietly.

'Try not to be too upset,' he began gently.

'Upset?' cried Jamie. 'Of course we're upset!'

'Please, try to understand Her Majesty's position.'

'What about Timber? What about us?'

'Yes, I know,' said Pendrick. 'Her Majesty is not herself anymore, but I can't believe she would ever harm Timber. He reminds her too much of Tyrus. But,' continued the wizard, 'do not attempt to remove that collar. It is the queen's collar to bewitch as she pleases and what is done, is done. All will come right in the end, I am sure.'

'What?' cried Jamie. 'How do you know?'

'Jamie,' interrupted Luke. 'I don't think we can change this.'

'If the wizards use memory mist on mum and dad, Luke's parents and Abigail's mum and granddad, and keep everyone else out of the way, well, then maybe we *can* do it,' said Jemima, hoping that magic would make everything right again.

'I think it sounds amazing,' said Abigail. The others looked at her.

'Aren't you even a little bit scared or worried?' asked Luke.

'Yes, I am,' said Abigail, 'but maybe we were meant to do it.'

The others kept staring at her. She was doing it again – saying strange things at strange times as if everything was normal.

'We succeeded the last time, even though we joined the quest very late and Timber and all the animals had done all the hard work,' said Abigail. Timber barked in agreement. 'This time we're in it right from the start, and, and …'

'And what?' asked Jamie, surprised by Abigail's ideas.

'And we've been asked by a queen to help her find a magic book to free her from a spell, save their magic and their world. Isn't that even a little bit amazing?'

'This is not going to be easy,' said Luke.

'Of course not, but we can do it with some help,' said Abigail.

'You're amazing,' said Jamie. 'How do you trust these people after what the queen just did?'

'They're trusting us with a lot, aren't they?' said Abigail.

'They are in a lot of trouble,' said Jemima.

'It sounds like they have a lot to lose if they don't get the WABOM back,' said Luke. 'They're counting on us.'

'Oh crikey,' sighed Jamie. 'Well, we absolutely have to do it to free Timber.' He looked at his dog. 'What do you think, boy?' Timber woo-wooed softly, like he always did when Jamie needed him. He rubbed his wet nose into Jamie's hands and licked his fingers, trying to tell him it would be OK.

'Good dog,' said Pendrick, patting him on the head. 'Now, everyone, follow me to the parlour. I think we could all do with some lemonade and cake!'

Chapter Six

MORE SECRETS

Timber led the way home to the hole beside the well in Grindlewood garden. When everyone had clambered up they went into the fairy house and shut the door. The garden residents were very keen to hear what had happened. Several of them moved closer to try to hear the conversation inside.

'What about that!' said Luke.

'We're right in the middle of a big magical problem again,' said Jemima.

'You mean, what about Timber and that thing around his neck,' said Jamie. 'How could she do that?'

'Remember what Professor Pendrick said,' said Luke. 'She sees Timber and thinks of her pet wolf. She won't hurt him, Jamie. She just wants to be sure we'll help her.'

'I hope you're right, but how do we do it?' said Jamie. 'Where do we start?'

'Hopefully they'll tell us when we get our instructions tomorrow,' said Luke.

Jemima took out the box from under the floorboards. 'I knew these treasures had to be magical,' she said, taking each piece out of the small wooden box and placing them carefully on the table.

'I don't see how a few bits of jewellery can help us find the most powerful magic book in the world – and save Timber,' said Jamie.

'You'll never lose Timber, Jamie,' said Abigail. 'We'll make sure of it.'

'Thanks,' muttered Jamie. Luke gave him a friendly dig. Jemima gave her brother a quick hug. Timber shoved his nose into his hand, then he barked. Dougal was scratching at the door. Several of the animals and birds were sitting on the porch waiting for Timber.

'I think we'll have plenty of help from our friends,' said Luke, opening the door wide. 'Look!'

Timber woofed softly and nodded to his friends. Dougal, Teddy, Eldric and Ramona came in and sat beside the children. The wood pigeons and robins fluttered in and perched on the book shelves. Cyril the heron landed on the windowsill.

'Wow,' said Jamie, beginning to smile. 'Looks like we have our own little army.'

'OK then,' said Luke. 'Are we ready for this quest?'

The children each put a hand on the lid of the wooden treasure box. In amongst the barks, meows and chirping, they each said loudly and bravely, 'Ready!'

❧

The Grindles had suggested to Abigail's mum that the two girls could have a joint birthday party in the Grindles' garden. As both Jemima and Abigail had birthdays in October, it seemed like a fun idea to invite all their friends for one big Halloween bash. The children were really looking forward to it and everyone was going to wear fancy dress. At least they had been looking forward to it, until they met the Forest Queen.

'Do you think the quest will be over before our party?' asked Jemima.

'I hope so,' said Abigail, 'but I'm not so sure.'

'How do we explain that we're on a mission to

find a magic book?' said Jamie.

'Let's hope Professor Pendrick can fix that problem, otherwise we'll be rightly stuck,' said Luke.

Jamie ran his hands through his floppy hair whenever he was cross or worried, and right now his hair looked like it had been electrified.

'I'm not sure I care what happens to that queen,' said Jamie. 'I just want to find the book and make sure Timber is safe.'

'They wouldn't have asked us if they didn't think we could do it, would they?' asked Abigail. No one answered that question.

'I always thought that magic was powerful and good and for ever and ...' Jemima didn't finish.

'And perfect?' said Luke. 'So did I, until I got caught in the middle of a feud! Never mind, it's still very special, and real, even if it's not perfect.'

Jemima tried to smile but she was disappointed that magic could cause so much trouble, and worse than that, some people wanted it for the wrong reasons.

Abigail's mum, Esther, had been chatting about the party with Jamie and Jemima's parents inside in the big house.

'Are you sure about the magic tricks?' asked Esther,

as they walked out to the garden together.

'I think the children will love it,' said Gloria.

'Are you worried about Mr Allnutt's magical ability?' chuckled Greg. He wondered if Abigail's granddad would be any good as a magician.

'Oh, he'll manage,' said Esther. 'I was just wondering if the children will like it, that's all.'

'Oh, they will, Esther,' said Gloria. 'The girls absolutely love anything to do with magic and Mr Allnutt has been so kind to give them all those lovely old books. Most of them seem to be about magic and spells and all that sort of thing. They keep the children amused for hours. And anyway, I'm looking forward to it too!'

'I'm sure Mr Allnutt will do a great job,' said Greg. 'I think Jemima might like to try some of those tricks herself!'

'Jamie and Luke are interested in all this magic stuff too, you know,' said Gloria.

'Well, I try to keep Abigail's feet on the ground, but children have great imaginations,' said Esther.

'Ah, here they are,' said Greg, 'in the fairy house as usual. I often wonder what they get up to in there.'

'Did you say *fairy* house?' asked Esther.

'That's what they wanted to call this tiny tumbledown cottage,' said Greg. 'No other name seemed quite right!'

'Goodness! Those three butterflies are absolutely huge,' said Esther, as they stood outside. The butterflies were sitting on the windowsill.

'They are extraordinary, aren't they?' said Gloria. 'They're almost the size of my hand.'

'Yes, indeed,' muttered Esther.

'We have some amazing wildlife here,' said Greg. 'The butterflies are one example, then there's the frog. The children call him Ernie. Amazingly, he has some sort of healing ability …'

Hearing their parents approach, the children quickly put the treasures away and ran outside. Timber and Dougal's barking and jumping distracted everyone while the fox ran off and Ramona bounced out the door. Esther watched the butterflies flutter off down the garden.

'Hi, Mum, hi, Dad,' said Jemima.

'Hello, Mrs Allnutt,' said Jamie. His mum peeped inside. 'Don't worry, Mum,' he said. 'The birds fly in and out, but they still nest in the trees like they always did.'

The smaller birds flew around Gloria and quickly returned to the treetops. The heron flew out the side window and perched elegantly on the roof.

'And what are you all up to today?' said Greg playfully.

'Nothing,' said Jamie a bit too quickly. 'We're, eh, we're going over to Luke's place, the farm, with the dogs, to see the chickens and the rooster, you know, to make sure they're settling in well.'

'Jamie, you mustn't worry about them so much,' said Gloria. 'They've been fine since we moved them over to the farm. The Finlays know how to look after them better than we do.'

'I'm sure they're much happier away from my noisy work shed,' said Greg.

'Right,' said Jamie.

'We're going to take Trigger for a walk too,' said Luke.

'Lovely,' said Gloria. 'Say hello to Mrs Finlay, won't you?'

'And please tell your Dad I'll be over later to help with the barn door,' said Greg.

'Sure, Mr Grindle,' said Luke.

'Is that a new collar on Timber?' asked Gloria.

'Um, it was a present, from eh, a friend,' muttered Jamie. They said some quick goodbyes and the four children hurried off to the barn to get the dogs' leashes.

Trigger was the Finlays' dog, a border collie. He worked with Luke's dad, Arthur, on the farm. His main job was to round up their new herd of sheep. He had helped defend Grindlewood garden from a dreadful attack by ferrets earlier in the year and was now good friends with the Grindles' dogs.

Timber and Dougal listened to the children chatter about the visit to Hollow Hill as they walked over to the Finlays' farmhouse. Dougal's eyes grew wider and wider and his floppy ears twitched as he took in every detail.

'This is incredible,' said Dougal. 'The others are going to be amazed when they hear all this. And that collar, Timber, how does it feel?'

'Just like a collar,' said Timber. 'A heavy collar. The queen thinks it's the only way to convince us to help her.'

'Oh, I see,' said Dougal, 'but wouldn't we have agreed to help anyway?'

'Of course,' replied Timber, 'but the queen couldn't be sure we would. Jamie's very upset about it, but I'm more concerned about what she's going to tell us tomorrow. I think it will be a difficult quest.'

'I hope we can do it,' said Dougal.

'So do I, Dougal,' said Timber, 'so do I.'

※

The Allnutts lived in the heart of Grindlewood village, where Esther was a history teacher in the local school. They lived with Abigail's granddad, Thaddeus Allnutt, who owned a little antiques shop. The family lived right beside the shop in a quaint house that was more than three hundred years old.

The cellar that Abigail often spoke of was full of strange and exciting things: old bits of gold and silver, ornaments, bronze artefacts, wood carvings, a large collection of paintings, etchings and mosaics, very old books, antique furniture waiting to be repaired and restored and many other odds and ends, most of which would never be sold in the shop. Many items were too old or battered to sell, according to Mr Allnutt, but he liked to keep them all, nonetheless. The shop was his business, the cellar his hobby, he said.

The shop was full of beautiful pieces and the Allnutts had made quite a name for themselves for having the best quality antiques for miles around. Thaddeus Allnutt was especially proud of his collection of old and unusual books, many of which he gave to Abigail to read, who in turn, shared them with her friends.

Esther was in quite a fuss by the time she got home from the Grindles'. The Allnutts' nightingale, Nura, was singing beautifully in her cage, but Esther was too flustered to notice.

'Thaddeus, we need to talk,' she said.

'Yes, dear, I know,' said Thaddeus. 'Have some tea. I just made a pot.'

'Thank you,' said Esther. 'Thaddeus, listen to me. I've seen the butterflies, the enchanted ones. They're in the Grindles' back garden. What are we going to do? They must be there for a reason.'

'Try to calm down, dear,' said her father-in-law. 'We knew someday that Grindlewood's secrets would start to unravel. They couldn't stay hidden for ever.'

'This is another sign, Thaddeus. Another trio of butterflies means more dark magic is afoot, more secrets will come out and then it will be harder to hide the truth from Abigail.'

'There was always the chance that she would find magic sooner or later,' said Thaddeus. 'Grindlewood is full of it. Perhaps it is time to tell her the whole story.'

'Do you think so? Oh, I don't know,' said Esther. 'When Edward was killed, I said I didn't want Abigail to have anything to do with magic. We came here to start a new life, away from all that.'

'Don't forget all the wonderful things that magic can do,' said Thaddeus. 'And look at Abigail – a beautiful Wandelei child, with a loving mother and granddad who will teach her well and keep her safe.'

'But the butterflies, Thaddeus, why do you think they are they back?'

'Wanda must have used a Phoenix Charm so that a new trio would be born once the old trio died,' said Thaddeus. 'I'm sure we'll find out why. All in good time.'

'And the queen – have you heard anything of her lately?' asked Esther. 'I've been afraid to ask any of our friends in the village about her. As you know, I've kept my distance these past few years.'

'I haven't heard anything, but I'll be meeting Pendrick soon,' said Thaddeus. 'I sent Nura with a message suggesting we meet.'

'Did you? Oh good. But what do you think I should do?' asked Esther. 'You know I want to do what's best for Abigail. I'm just not sure what that is.'

'Dearest Esther, you know what I think. I believe she should be told who she is and all that it means – and before her ninth birthday, so that she may learn magic if she wants to. We are also responsible for protecting and continuing our magic and our traditions, as you well know.'

'Oh dear,' said Esther. 'I know she must begin her training on her ninth birthday, or she will never be able to practise magic. But that leaves so little time to decide what to do, and what if the butterflies are here for something important, even dangerous? I suppose I was hoping I would never have to make this decision. I've thought about it so many times and I still don't know what to do.' Esther finally took a breath.

'Calm yourself,' said Thaddeus. 'I think we should prepare her for whatever lies ahead.' He took hold of Esther's hands. 'I have no doubt that telling her the truth is the right thing to do, but she only needs three lessons before her birthday to fulfil the obligation. We have a little over a week to think about it and decide once and for all.'

Chapter Seven

PREPARING FOR THE QUEST

Word was sent around to all the garden residents that another meeting would be held after dark. They gathered near the big granite stone at the end of the garden. Timber was just about to begin, when Dougal barked. 'Look, here they come!'

Everyone looked up as the snowy owl circled down, followed closely by the sparrows and blackbirds. They flew straight over to the gathering.

'Hello, everyone,' tooted the owl, landing in their midst.

'Welcome home!' said Timber.

The little birds perched on a few low branches. As usual, Oberon sat on the grass. They were all tired out, so Timber began the meeting by explaining his strange afternoon in Hollow Hill.

'Wow!' said Ramona. 'You really met the queen!'

'Was it scary seeing her stuck in the ground like that?' purred Cindy.

'It was definitely strange,' said Timber. 'This is the collar she put on me.' He shook his head and the collar glistened in the moonlight.

'Oh dear, how dreadful,' said the Brigadier. 'Can we do anything about it?'

'No,' replied Timber. 'The queen will only remove it when we complete the quest. If we fail, the collar will keep me in Hollow Hill, or choke me if I try to leave.'

'But you're trying to help her!' said Eldric.

'This sounds dreadful,' said the frog. 'You're going to need everyone to help you on the quest. What can I do, Timber, now that my healing powers are gone?'

'Don't worry, Ernie,' said Timber, 'there'll be something for everyone to do. Some of you will stay here to keep an eye on the garden. Others will come on the quest with me and the children – but not everyone.'

'What about Gildevard?' asked Teddy. 'Does he know about this?'

'Do we even know where he is?' asked Norville.

'We don't know where he is and we never know what he's up to,' said Timber. 'As for the queen, she thinks we are her last hope. She knows we defeated Worfeus and that's why she trusts us to find and return the WABOM,' said Timber.

'How did we ever get involved in quests?' asked the Brigadier. 'Life used to be very simple around here, until, eh, until –'

'Until we arrived?' said Timber, grinning at his old friend. 'By the sounds of it, Grindlewood will be in a lot of trouble if the Wandeleis don't find their magic book.'

'What are the children saying about all this?' asked Oberon.

'First they were surprised, then a little shocked, now I think they're worried. We'll be working closely together this time,' said Timber. 'The professors said they will use memory mist on the non-magical people so they won't remember any magic they might see. Even the children's parents won't know what's going on.'

'Timber told me earlier that some of the treasures have magic that can help us,' said Dougal.

'So they do contain magic,' said Cindy.

'That's right. The queen will explain the treasures tomorrow too,' said Timber.

The meeting quietened down. There was a lot happening all of a sudden and everyone needed to think about it.

'Luckily, the children are on their mid-term break from school,' said Ramona after a moment or two.

'Let's hope the quest is over quickly,' said Norville. 'They only have a week off.'

'The professors said something about time-twisting,' said Timber, 'though I'm not sure how that will work.'

'Is that so?' said Eldric. 'Will time be longer or shorter or just different?'

'Em, I don't know, but I'm sure it will all be explained,' said Timber, turning to the owl. 'Now, tell us what happened up north, Oberon. I'm glad you made it back safe and sound.'

'As you know, we've had our suspicions about Bodric,' said the owl, 'and I'm afraid we were right. He is also after the WABOM, on behalf of a sorceress called Zora.'

The residents groaned.

'And he knows that the Forest Queen is looking for it too.'

'Hmm, that could make things more complicated,' said Timber.

'Sounds like we're in a race,' said Dougal.

'Then it's good to know who our competitors are,' said Eldric.

'Don't you mean enemies?' said Norville. 'I think this quest just became a lot more dangerous.'

'Well, we'll just have to win the race and take the prize,' said Timber. 'That's all for now, everyone. We'll talk again tomorrow when we get back from Hollow Hill. Get some rest and prepare for quest number two. Goodnight.'

All the residents wished each other good luck and goodnight and went on their way. Timber, Dougal and Teddy went off on garden patrol. Later, after Timber gave his final howl to the night, all was quiet in Grindlewood – before the next quest.

❧

'Did you have any trouble getting here?' asked Jemima as she opened the hall door. It was still dark outside.

'No,' said Abigail. 'Granddad was up early and offered to drive me over.'

'Gee, that was lucky,' said Jamie. 'I guess the mesmerising has begun.'

'Here's Luke,' called Jemima, pointing at Luke free-wheeling down the long driveway on the bicycle he got for his tenth birthday that summer.

'Hi there!' called Luke.

'Bring the bike around to the side gate,' Jamie called, before running around to open it. 'I was hoping you wouldn't be asked to do any chores this morning.'

'No, it was fine,' said Luke. 'I was meant to help Dad with a few things, but he just waved me off! Trigger followed me to the farm gate and kept barking like mad. I think he knows we're up to something.'

'Well, we might need him,' said Jamie. Timber barked. 'Yep, I think Timber would like to have Trigger around.'

'Let's see what happens this morning,' said Luke.

The four children went to the fairy house. Timber and Teddy followed.

'Right, let's take the treasures out,' said Jamie.

'Here we are, the ring, the brooch, the string with coloured stones, the tiara, the gold key and … should we bring the crystal key as well?' asked Jemima.

'Maybe not,' said Jamie.

'The queen didn't actually ask for it,' said Luke.

'That's true,' said Jemima. 'We'll leave it here.'

Jemima put the items carefully back in the small jewelled box and Jamie placed the crystal key on its own under the floorboards.

'We should go now,' said Luke.

They left the fairy house in silence and walked over to the tunnel.

'Let's try not to get so mucky this time,' said Jemima.

Jamie had just slid down to the top of the ladder and Luke was half in and half out of the hole when they stopped.

'The butterflies are coming,' cried Abigail. 'They must have something to tell us.'

Two butterflies landed in the girls' hair and one flew over to Timber. The boys waited as the girls and Timber listened to the message.

'They want some of the animals to come too,' said Jemima.

'Which ones?' asked Jamie. Timber barked a few times. He had received the same message and was telling the others. Teddy, Dougal, Eldric and Ramona moved forward and stood beside Timber.

'I guess they're coming with us,' said Jamie.

'Yes, they are,' said Abigail, beaming. It was the first time the butterflies had given her a message.

'Come on, Timber, you first,' said Jamie, but Timber was still barking.

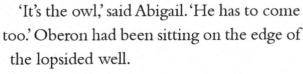 'It's the owl,' said Abigail. 'He has to come too.' Oberon had been sitting on the edge of the lopsided well.

'Are you sure they want so many of us to go?' tooted the owl.

'The butterflies just said so,' barked Timber.

'I guess that makes sense,' said Abigail.

'What does?' asked Jamie.

'The butterflies told Timber, so he could tell the animals and birds,' explained Abigail. 'Then the butterflies told us, so we wouldn't try to stop them.'

'But why so many?' said Jamie.

'Maybe they'll be needed,' said Luke.

Jamie looked anxiously at his friend, then at the pets. He stroked Timber's ears and patted Dougal on the head. 'Come on, then. Let's go.'

The boys helped Timber down first, followed

quickly by Teddy, who nimbly ran down the ladder by himself. Jamie came back up to help Dougal, Luke lifted Eldric to the ground after he had slid half way down the ladder, and Ramona managed to bounce down before skidding to a halt. Oberon flew down after the girls as the rest of the residents watched from the garden and wished them good luck.

The group set off down the tunnel. The three enchanted butterflies fluttered just ahead of them, leading the way through the tunnels lit with gold and on to Hollow Hill. The quest had begun. There was no turning back.

Chapter Eight

THE QUEEN'S TREASURES

When they arrived at the royal chamber, the queen was in a rage. Ripley was sitting in a pile of nuts, tucked in at the foot of the tree, well clear of the queen's wildly waving branches. He sniggered at the professors who looked tired and frustrated.

'Why do you keep asking me this question?' roared the queen. 'I will not announce my successor until we have the WABOM.'

'Successor?' whispered Luke, nudging Jamie with his elbow.

Jamie shrugged his shoulders. The children looked at each other, wondering what to do. They had arrived at an awkward moment.

'Your Majesty, the children, Timber and the other animals and a white owl are here,' said Pendrick.

'What? Oh, yes, good,' said the queen, still cross. 'Well? Did you bring the treasures?'

'Here they are,' said Jemima, holding up the wooden box.

'Bring it to me,' said the queen. 'Open it and put it on the ground.' Jemima obeyed. The queen swept her branches down and lifted each piece in turn with her leaf-hands. 'Come closer, all of you. Ripley, that's enough crunching.' The squirrel spat out his nut and stared at the box.

'Timber,' whispered Ramona. 'I think I've seen that squirrel before, in our rabbit fields.'

'I've seen him too,' whispered Eldric. 'He was running around our forest a couple of weeks ago. I thought he was gathering nuts, but maybe not.'

'He's a sneaky one,' growled Timber. 'Watch him closely.'

The queen began her explanation of the treasures.

'I gave these jewels to Wanda before she left in search of new magic and the WABOM,' said the queen. 'This is the Brooch of Balmedoch.' She held up the brooch with the dark-red stone. 'It is the most complex of all the treasures. The four diamonds around the edge of the garnet are part of its time-twisting compass. They will take you to where the four parts of the WABOM are located. This only works if they are located directly north, south, east and west of Hollow Hill. The augurers assure me that all four books are in those locations now, although they cannot say *exactly* where. You will have to find them.'

Jamie was about to protest when the professors interrupted.

'You may visit some rather unusual places with this brooch, places that are not always on normal, that is, non-magical maps,' said Sparks, taking the brooch from the queen and showing it to the children.

'What does she mean by time-twisting?' said Timber, looking at Oberon.

'I don't know,' tooted the owl. 'It must be able to transport us through time as well as space, sort of.'

'Or another dimension,' muttered Eldric. 'How extraordinary!'

'Ahem, to use the brooch correctly,' said Sparks, looking from one animal to the other and then back to the children, 'you must draw a circle, decide where you are going and pull out the correct diamond.'

The children and the pets stared at him.

'It's not that complicated,' said Flint. 'There are only four diamonds on the brooch, representing north, south, east and west.'

'For example,' said Pendrick, 'let's say you want to go north. First, pull out this pin at the back of the brooch and draw a circle on the ground around all those who will be travelling.'

'Then, gently pull out the diamond that points to where you want to go – north, south, east or west,' said Sparks. 'This one here is for north.' He pointed to one of the diamonds. 'There's a tiny *n* engraved just beneath it. You can see it right here.'

'Gently does it – it must not detach,' added Flint. He pulled the diamond and the dark-red stone immediately reacted. It swirled clockwise just once, then stopped. 'Once the circle is drawn, the diamond is chosen and pulled out, *and* the garnet is spinning continuously, you will be transported to your destination.'

'As space and time will be altered, you may find you lose more brooch hours than you might expect,' said Sparks. 'This is particularly important to remember, so that you do not waste time – time you haven't got.'

'Huh?' said Jamie.

'What are brooch hours?' asked Luke.

'Actually, we aren't sure,' said Sparks. 'Brooch hours can't be measured accurately. You will have to rely on your own watch!'

'What the professor means is that it would be wise not to waste any time,' said Pendrick. 'Whoever is drawing the circle must remember to jump *inside* the circle before pulling the diamond out, otherwise he or she will be left behind, and those who have departed may not be able to return without the brooch.'

'It can be rather startling the first time, so make sure you are holding hands or paws, or whatever,' said Sparks. Oberon tooted and glared at him. 'The birds should probably sit on your shoulders or arms and hold on tight.'

'Seriously?' said Jamie. 'We have to hold on to the pets to make sure we don't lose them?'

'O – K,' said Luke, wondering if it could ever work without a hitch.

'Oh,' said both girls quietly, hoping they wouldn't end up stranded somewhere weird and never return.

'How do we get back?' asked Luke.

'I'm glad you asked that,' whispered Jemima.

'Excellent question,' said Sparks. 'You do the reverse – draw another circle and push the diamond back *in*. The brooch will take you back to where you started.'

'Balmedoch was always inventing clever things,' said Flint excitedly. 'Sparks and I were his apprentices, eh, a long time ago, of course.'

'Yes, a complex wizard, if ever there was one,' muttered Pendrick, as he pinned the brooch on Jemima's collar. 'You have a wide collar on your coat, Jemima, and this pin is very strong. It should sit there without falling off. You must travel at exactly seven in the morning and return before the last stroke of seven in the evening, or you will have to wait until the next portal opens – the next day.'

'Portal?' muttered Jamie. Luke raised his eyebrows. So, portals were real. The children exchanged several glances. They wanted to ask more questions but the queen seemed to be in a hurry.

'Next, we have Gorlan's ring. Gorlan was a famous warrior, a great swordsman. This ring is a true treasure, uncomplicated and pure. You will know the ring has accepted you when –'

This time Jamie interrupted.

'When you can see a gold cross in the centre of the blue stone?'

'That's right,' said the queen. 'Put it on, Jamie.'

Jamie put the ring on the middle finger of his right hand. The cross shone brightly. The professors looked surprised, but pleased.

'It seems the ring has already chosen you, Jamie,' said the queen. 'This is a good omen.'

'If you are in danger, the ring will turn even a toy sword into the lightest but strongest piece of steel – a real sword,' said Pendrick. 'Make sure you wear this ring and bring your wooden sword with you.'

Jamie stared at him. How did Pendrick know he had a wooden sword? It had been a present for his sixth birthday, nearly five years ago.

'With this ring on your finger, you will fight like a true swordsman, just like Gorlan,' said Sparks excitedly. Jamie looked at Sparks. Suddenly the quest was sounding very serious.

'Sword fighting? But …' Jamie mumbled, trying to imagine fighting like a warrior called Gorlan.

'Now, the String of Charms,' said the queen, holding it up. 'These seven gemstones are magical, but there are rules. Once you make a wish, you cannot change it. You cannot wish for something entirely selfish, nor can you wish for the same thing twice. Each gemstone may only be used once, in strict sequence, and only on this quest, then its power is spent.'

'But how do we make the magic happen?' asked Luke.

'Starting with the emerald,' said Pendrick, 'unclip the stone, hold it tightly in your hand and wish for what you need. Do not think of anything else. If your wish is not clear to the charm, the magic will be lost.'

'Any one of you can use these stones, but one of you should wear the string until they are all used up,' said Flint.

'Take it, Luke,' said the queen.

'Tie it around your wrist and pull your sleeve down over it,' said Pendrick, taking the string from the queen and handing it to Luke. 'It is best kept hidden.'

'Guard it well,' said the queen. 'Any magical being will know those gemstones and what they can do.'

Jamie helped Luke secure it tightly around his wrist.

'Do you understand everything so far?' The queen looked at each of the children, then at all the animals and the owl, one by one. Each nodded back. 'Good. You have no need of the gold key on this quest. It will remain here.'

Ripley scampered over to the box, picked up the key, then ran up the queen's trunk and sat down near her head.

'Thank you, my squirrel. Now give the key to Pendrick.'

'But Lyra, don't you want to keep it close?' said Ripley. 'Will I mind it for you?'

'I will keep it safe, Your Majesty,' said Pendrick quickly, holding out his hand. None of the professors wanted Ripley to have the key.

'Thank you, Pendrick,' said the queen. 'Ripley, put it in the box for the professor.'

The squirrel reluctantly obeyed. Pendrick picked up the box and held on to it.

'Where is the crystal key?' asked the queen sharply. 'I am told you have it also.'

'You didn't ask us to bring it,' said Luke quickly.

'We need that key to conduct the Renewal Charm,' said the queen.

'We'll bring it to you after the quest, when you release Timber,' said Jamie.

The queen was about to explode with rage when Pendrick intervened.

'Your Majesty,' he said, 'the children have kept it safe until now and we won't need it until the WABOM is returned. The garden itself is not under threat so it should be safe.'

'Very well,' said the queen with a loud sigh. 'Bring it to me at the end of the quest.'

'Yes, Your Majesty,' said Pendrick, on the children's behalf. He shook his head to discourage any further comments.

'But what if we need to use it?' said Abigail, ignoring the professor.

'Abigail, I heard that you recognised the power of the crystal key,' said the queen, lowering her head as far as she could. 'You show great intuition, my dear. But no, you will not take it with you. We must renew our magic very soon and we cannot risk it falling into enemy hands. You have the other treasures to help you.'

'What about the tiara?' asked Jemima.

'The Tiara Lei,' said the queen, correcting her. 'You

have no need of it either. It will only fit the head of a potential Wandelei queen.'

The queen, the professors and even the squirrel noticed how the boys and Jemima immediately turned towards Abigail.

'What is this? I sense some disturbance,' said the queen. 'It is too late to have doubts. This is your quest and you must succeed.'

'Your Majesty, we still need to explain the four parts of the WABOM and where they are located,' said Sparks, trying to distract the queen from another fit of rage.

The queen's face twitched as she stared at Abigail, wondering what it was about the girl that intrigued her. Abigail felt very uncomfortable, but after a minute or two, the queen calmed down.

'The three Grindlewood butterflies have already charmed your parents, have they not?' she said.

'Em, we think so,' said Luke.

'Well then, don't worry about your normal lives. As you have seen, my butterflies will enchant your families, teachers, friends and anyone else they have to, to allow you to do what you must. Elsewhere, wizards and witches will use memory mist to keep this quest a secret.'

'What do you mean, "do what we must"?' asked Jamie.

'And where is "elsewhere"?' asked Luke.

'Do not question me!' roared the queen.

'Stop shouting at us! We'll do our best to help you – oh!' cried Abigail suddenly, surprising even herself.

'Well said, Abby,' whispered Jamie.

The queen stared at her, her eyes blazing, but then a thought struck her and her expression changed. Jamie jumped forward, thinking the queen was about to strike, but she just kept staring at Abigail, her long, straight black hair, large green eyes and delicate stature.

'Lotus, tell the augurers I wish to see them, now,' said the queen to her fairy-in-waiting.

'Yes, Your Majesty.' Lotus left the chamber.

The professors looked uneasy. Jamie remained in front of Abigail and then Jemima began pleading with the queen.

'Abigail's right. You don't have to be so angry. We're happy to help and we know this quest is very important. We'll do our best, honestly we will, but don't threaten us – it's not fair.'

'Well said, Jem!' said Jamie.

'Yes, well done,' whispered Luke.

Abigail squeezed Jemima's hand and smiled weakly at her. The queen let out a long, sad sigh. Perhaps she had been unfair. Perhaps she should stop doubting the children and the animals, but she was frustrated and anxious, and curious about something – Abigail. The girl looked like a Wandelei and spoke like a Wandelei.

'I apologise,' said the queen. 'Come forward, Abigail. Don't be afraid.'

Abigail moved slowly and Jamie moved with her, keeping Timber close.

'Put on the tiara, dear,' said the queen.

Abigail froze. Pendrick took the tiara out of the box and placed it on her head. It fit. The professors took in sharp breaths. Lotus gave a stifled shriek as she re-entered the room with the five augurers. The queen sighed again and smiled.

'So,' she said, 'the Tiara Lei does fit you. What is your family name, Abigail? Who are your parents?'

'My mum's name is Esther, but I don't remember my dad. He died when I was two. His name was Edward, Edward Allnutt.'

'Esther? Edward?' muttered the queen, trying to remember.

'Allnutt?' cried Pendrick. 'Do you know a Thaddeus Allnutt?'

'Yes,' said Abigail. 'He's my granddad.'

'Oh my,' said Flint, almost fainting.

'Goodness gracious!' muttered Sparks.

'Do you know him?' asked Abigail.

'Oh, perhaps,' muttered Pendrick. 'Yes, I think we may have met somewhere, here and there, round and about.'

'Well, well,' said the queen. 'Secrets will come out. Return the tiara to the box, dear. We will talk about this another time.' Abigail obeyed but her mind was spinning. She stood beside her friends, trembling. Jemima put her arm around her.

'Timber, come to me,' said the queen.

'What do you want him for?' cried Jamie.

'Be still, Jamie,' said the queen crossly. 'Not all animals can speak to me, but I will enchant Timber so that he can tell me of the quest each time you return. Tyrus used to talk to me.'

She waved her arms and cast a spell over Timber before anyone could say or do anything.

The five augurers shuffled forward in their long grey cloaks. They bowed before the queen.

'Augurers, take the Tiara Lei and let me know your findings,' said the queen. 'I want to know how many potential queens there are.'

One of the augurers took the tiara. All five of them noticed Abigail and they continued staring and whispering as they left the chamber.

'Timber, come sit by me,' said the queen. 'Pendrick, explain the WABOM.'

Timber trotted over and sat down beside the queen's lumpy roots. Luke held Jamie's arm and shook his head. Now wasn't the time to argue with the queen. She was in a bad mood and they had a lot to learn about the quest.

Chapter Nine

THE WABOM

'Perhaps we should all sit down,' said Pendrick. With a single swish from his wand, the chairs that stood around the edges of the chamber whisked into the centre of the room. The three professors and four children sat down. The dogs and Eldric sat at their feet. Teddy sat on Jemima's lap, Ramona hopped into Abigail's arms, while Oberon seemed content to perch on Luke's shoulder.

'*The Wandeleis' Ancient Book of Magic* – the WABOM – is a book, made up of four books: *The Book of Light*, *The Book of Darkness*, *The Book of Wisdom* and *The Book of Potions and Spells*,' said Pendrick. 'On the day Her Majesty was cursed, the Worfagons stole the WABOM. Certain brave warriors came to our aid and returned it to us. However, the Worfagons were furious and laid siege to what remained of the palace. The queen ordered four wizards to each take one part of the WABOM, go into hiding and not to return until it was safe.'

'Since that day, at least two of those wizards have been confirmed dead and we lost touch with the other two,' said Sparks. 'Only recently, the augurers have been able to confirm, through their mystical practices, that each part of the WABOM now lies due north, south, east and west from here, Her Majesty's *temporary* palace.'

'The four points of the compass, like the compass brooch,' said Jemima.

'Exactly,' said Flint.

'But if you know where the books are, why don't you just get them?' asked Jamie crossly.

'Silence!' roared the queen. 'I have already explained that.'

'It was decreed by the Ancients that if we were to lose the WABOM, we must request someone else to return it,' said Pendrick. 'It is one of the conditions of ownership, and a type of punishment for losing it in the first place.'

'How dangerous is this going to be?' asked Luke.

There was a short and awkward silence.

'It won't be easy,' said Flint, 'but you were successful on the first quest, and I'm sure that surprised you, ahem.'

'Yes, thank you, Professor Flint,' said Pendrick. Sparks frowned at Flint.

'Great,' said Jamie. 'And how are we supposed to know where to look, if the augurers can't agree on exactly where each book is?'

'Maybe we'll know when we get there,' whispered Jemima weakly.

'Really?' said Jamie. Luke was frowning. He didn't like to say it but he wasn't sure they would succeed. It was sounding more dangerous and complicated by the minute.

'Perhaps the magic will guide us,' said Abigail after a moment. 'Remember your ring, Jamie, how it chose you and what it can do. And we have the magic of the other treasures too. That might be all we need.'

'I hope you're right,' said Jamie. 'You make it sound better anyway.'

He looked at Gorlan's ring on his finger. To his surprise he rather liked it. The gold cross in the centre was throbbing brightly inside the blue stone.

'OK,' said Jamie. 'Let's hear the rest of it.'

'We understand from the augurers,' said Flint, 'that *The Book of Potions and Spells* is in the east, possibly very near Grindlewood village, or forest, or –'

'Or somewhere *east* of Hollow Hill,' added Pendrick. 'We would like you to look for *The Book of Potions and Spells* first, so that once you return it we can speed up our work on a spell to free Her Majesty.'

'Also, the augurers don't think anyone is guarding it,' added Flint.

'Guarding it?' said Luke. 'Are the books guarded?'

'Possibly,' said Sparks. 'Well, probably, and there may be others looking for the WABOM, so don't trust anyone.'

Timber and Dougal growled. Teddy hissed.

'Don't be alarmed,' said Pendrick. '*The Book of Light* is also close by, slightly south of here according to our learned friends, but there seems to be some sort of protective shield around it.'

'Do you mean it's protected by magic?' asked Jemima.

'Well, it might be,' said Pendrick.

'Huh? How do we …?' began Jamie.

'What is *The Book of Light* for?' asked Abigail.

'That's a bit difficult to explain,' said the queen, interrupting. 'Please continue Pendrick.'

'*The Book of Wisdom* is in the west, and *The Book of Darkness* is north.'

'*The Book of Darkness*?' said Jamie. 'That sounds bad.'

'It contains dark magic,' said Audmund, one of the augurers. He had returned to the chamber after examining the tiara. From under his hooded cloak, his silver eyes bulged with interest as he listened to the conversation.

'They're right about it being in the north,' tooted the owl.

Timber explained to the queen what they knew from Bodric's camp.

'I'm glad you can confirm its whereabouts,' said the queen. 'The augurers had great difficulty locating *The Book of Darkness* for some reason, but we have known for some time that *The Book of Wisdom* is in the west. The Crabbage Crones have it. They keep it in one of their caves where they live as outcasts. It is rumoured that some demented character gave it to them in return for a love potion. What nonsense!'

'The crones still have it,' croaked Audmund. 'We saw it in our trance.'

'Yes, thank you, Audmund,' said Pendrick, turning back to the group. 'The Crabbage Crones are ghastly old witches who were cast out long ago for breaking the rules of magic. They live in the remotest and grimmest surroundings. You will certainly need your sword out there, Jamie.'

'And arrows,' said Phineas, another augurer, who was shuffling behind Audmund. 'Arrows work well against the crones.'

The queen waved her leaf-hand and dismissed the augurers.

'Now,' said Pendrick, 'to find *The Book of Potions and Spells* you must journey east with the compass. We think that Worfeus had this book when he was stuck in Grindlewood Forest. He would have needed it to reverse the curses that Wanda put on him.'

'You mean the forest behind our garden?' said Jamie.

'Yes, the very same,' said Pendrick.

'Grindlewood Forest is also east of Hollow Hill, you see, so it is certainly a possibility,' added Flint.

'Ripley went to look for the book in there but he didn't find it, though it might be worth checking it again,' said Pendrick as he frowned.

'He went looking without permission,' said Sparks quietly, shaking his head.

'But it is more likely to be in another forest, also east of here, and, eh, surprisingly close,' said Flint.

'What? Where?' asked Jamie.

'Oh, it's not on any normal map,' said Flint.

'The compass will show you,' said Pendrick.

'So the brooch doesn't take us to *normal* places, only *magical* places, is that it?' asked Luke.

'The Brooch of Balmedoch can take you anywhere,' said Sparks.

The children exchanged confused glances. Timber growled and looked at Sparks for further explanation, but all he got was a watery smile. Timber barked a few times at the queen and she replied to everyone.

'Timber thinks you should search both forests at the same time. It's a good idea. Go now. Once you find each part of the WABOM you must return it to me at once. And do *not* use the crystal key. Once upon a time, there were several crystal keys, but they were often *lost* and *misused*, so I confiscated them. This one is special. It must not be lost or misused. Is that clear?'

The children nodded.

'One other thing,' said the queen. 'Wanda knew that if a group of wildlife and pets could live so honourably, they could be trusted with anything, even our magic and our secrets. We Wandeleis live by a similar code of honour and trust. Remember this when the quest frightens or confounds you. Our worlds are closer and more entwined than you know.'

As they left the queen's chamber, the children were very quiet. The queen's parting words had been especially worrying.

The animals were less bothered. They were keen to return to Grindlewood to tell the others everything and to set off to the forests to begin the search.

'By the way,' said Pendrick as he walked back to the reception chamber with them, 'I have organised an extra bit of tunnel for you. It should be more convenient than using the hole beside the well. You might meet our friendly diggers on your way back. Don't forget to thank them. They like to be appreciated. Good luck tomorrow!'

'I wonder who told him about the mucky hole,' said Luke.

'Probably the butterflies,' said Jemima. 'Or maybe he just noticed our clothes.'

'They'll be keeping an eye on us, won't they?' said Abigail.

'I hope so,' muttered Jamie.

The children didn't talk much on the way back. Their heads were buzzing with thoughts of magic and spells and the four locations of the WABOM, not to mention space and time-twisting portals and the magic of the treasures.

'I know I asked you before, but do you *really* think we can do it, Timber?' asked Dougal, trotting beside him.

'Yes, Dougal,' said the malamute. 'It will be quite an adventure, but we can do it.'

'I think it sounds complicated,' said Eldric. 'How much time do we have?'

'The queen didn't exactly say, but I get the feeling it isn't much,' said Timber.

'Well, at least we know where to start – in the forests,' said Teddy.

'We'll split into two groups,' said Timber. 'One group will search the nearby forest and one will go by magical compass. That'll save time.'

'Right,' said Dougal. 'Who's in each group?'

'I think Cindy, Eldric, Ramona and a few of the other rabbits should search Grindlewood Forest.' Timber looked at the fox. 'You know it very well, Eldric. Search it thoroughly.'

'Will do,' said Eldric.

'Teddy, Dougal, Trigger, Oberon and I will go with the children to the other forest – the one not on any normal map.'

'Let's hope we find the first book quickly and we can move on to the next one,' said Dougal.

'Maybe some of the birds could help too,' said Teddy.

'Yes, we'll divide the birds into search teams as well, but some of them should stay in the garden,' said Timber.

'Perhaps the blackbirds and sparrows could scout around in Grindlewood Forest,' said Oberon. 'They did a good job with me up north.'

'Good idea,' said Timber.

The animals chattered quietly amongst themselves

most of the way home. The children were distracted by their own thoughts and concerns until they were interrupted by loud, out-of-tune singing.

'What is making that awful racket?' said Luke.

As they rounded a bend in the tunnel, they got quite a surprise. Two dwarfs were heading in the opposite direction, merrily singing and banging their shovels on the way back to Hollow Hill. Professor Pendrick had asked the two brothers to extend the tunnel as far as the fairy house to make it easier for the children to travel in and out. Once an enormous reward meal was mentioned, the two beefy dwarfs, Jugjaw and Bushfire, were only too happy to oblige.

'Eh, hello there,' said Jamie.

'Hi ho,' said one.

'Howdy,' said the other.

'We've just finished a new piece of tunnel for you. Hope you like it!' said the first one.

'Oh, thank you very much,' said Jemima, remembering what the professor had said.

'Thanks very much, guys,' said Luke.

The two dwarfs smiled broadly but didn't stop.

'I'm Bushfire, and this here is my brother, Jugjaw.

Make sure you remember who's who! We don't like it when folks muddle us up,' called Bushfire, as they marched past.

There was little chance of that. If Jugjaw was the one with the huge square jaw, then his brother was obviously the one with hair and a beard that looked like a bush on fire. The dwarfs tipped their caps as they passed Abigail.

'Hello,' said Abigail shyly. 'Thank you very much, both of you.'

'You're welcome,' said Jugjaw.

'Good luck with the quest,' called Bushfire. 'We're counting on you!' His booming voice echoed through the tunnel.

'Counting on us!' said Jamie.

'No pressure, then,' said Luke. He grinned at Jamie, who shook his floppy hair and smiled back. They were quiet again until Abigail needed to say something.

'Look, I don't know why that tiara fits me, or how the professors know of my granddad, or why those two dwarfs tipped their hats like that, really I don't. It's a complete mystery to me.'

'I think it's great!' said Jemima. 'It means you could be a witch, or a queen-in-waiting, or both, and then you could learn magic. How brilliant!'

'Is it? I'm not sure,' said Abigail. 'We don't really know, do we? I might ask Granddad later, maybe, maybe not, I don't know.'

'But you can't ask him, or tell him,' said Luke. 'It's got to be a secret. Even if the memory mist is used to wipe everyone's memories, we have to keep quiet about all this, it's too, too –'

'Crazy?' said Jamie. 'You bet it is, but I think Abby might have to talk to someone,' he said quietly to Luke.

'I suppose,' muttered Luke.

'Don't worry, Abby,' said Jamie, 'no matter what the professors and your granddad say, we're still your friends, right?'

'Thanks, Jamie,' said Abigail, but what bothered her most was that she had never heard anything about this from her own family. Timber trotted beside her and gave her a few licks. Ramona bounded over so that Abigail would pick her up again and cuddle her. She snuggled into her arms and looked up at her with big soft eyes. Abigail smiled and rubbed the rabbit's ears.

'See, all the animals agree,' said Jemima.

'Hey, we're back!' cried Luke.

'Look at the new tunnel!' cried Jamie. 'They've

moved the ladder over from the hole to the new bit they dug out. Now we can go straight into the fairy house and come up through the floor. This is cool.'

'They've put in a trap door, with a lock and a mat to cover it,' said Luke, pushing up the trap door. He moved the mat aside and climbed up into the fairy house. The others followed. Jamie looked at the carpentry. He was impressed.

'They've added a couple of steps and made them wider so the animals can get up and down easily,' he said. 'This is really good.'

When everyone was up, the animals followed Timber outside. They had to tell the rest of the residents about their plan. The children stayed in the fairy house.

'Right,' said Jamie, 'let's check everything again.'

'Don't forget your sword,' said Abigail. Jamie strapped his wooden sword securely around his waist.

'And the bow and arrows,' said Jemima, handing Jamie's set to Luke.

'You don't mind me using your arrows as well, do you, Jamie? I think we should bring lots.'

'Sure,' said Jamie. 'I'm bringing a map and a torch too.'

'And the treasures?' said Luke.

Jemima checked to make sure the brooch was still on her collar. Luke showed them the String of Charms around his wrist and Jamie put out his hand with Gorlan's ring.

'What'll I bring?' asked Abigail.

Suddenly they realised that Abigail was the only one not carrying a treasure, or anything at all.

'How about *The Book of Enchantments*?' said Jamie. 'That came in handy before.'

'Yes, why didn't I think of it?' said Abigail. She took the little book off the shelf behind her and stuffed it in her coat pocket.

'OK then, that's everything sorted in here,' said Jamie. 'Timber is organising the animals outside.' They went to the little window. There was a lot of sniffing, tail-wagging and feather-fluttering as the residents discussed the plan. They were excited by the news and impressed that Timber could now speak witch language.

'It's a little weird,' said Timber. 'I hardly even know I'm doing it, but it could come in useful.'

'It certainly could,' said Oberon. 'Mine is a little rusty.'

'What did the queen say when she first spoke to you in witch language?' asked the Brigadier.

'She talked a little about Wanda,' said Timber. 'She cared a great deal for her, and apparently Wanda had six older sisters. The eldest was Esther, Abigail's mother, which means Wanda was Abigail's aunt.'

'That means Abigail is a Wandelei witch!' said the Brigadier. 'Does she know?'

'I don't think so,' said Timber, 'but she must be wondering about it. Now, we know Worfeus made a lot of potions when he was stuck in Grindlewood Forest, so it's possible he was using *The Book of Potions and Spells* while he was in there.'

'We'll be sure to search it thoroughly,' said Eldric.

'Let's hope travelling by magical brooch isn't too uncomfortable,' said Dougal.

'It sounds more like a time-tunnel than a time-twister,' said Oberon.

'What's the difference?' asked Teddy. 'Never mind, I think it'll be fun!'

'That's the spirit!' said Timber. 'Come on, it's time for food. We'll be leaving early in the morning so make sure you're all ready to go.'

Chapter Ten

THE BOOK OF POTIONS AND SPELLS

Early the next morning, Timber called his friends to begin the quest.

'AROO-WOO-WOO, AROO-WOO-WOO!'

They waited by the fairy house for the children. Luke cycled over and this time he brought Trigger with him. Jamie let them in through the side gate and Trigger charged around the garden, leaping and bounding about with excitement. The other residents were delighted to see him.

'Good boy, Trigger,' said Jamie, trying to pat the energetic dog.

'Hey, here's Abigail!' said Jemima.

'Hi,' said Abigail, panting. 'I had to take the bus this time. I was worried I might be late so I ran all the way up the avenue. Phew!'

'We still have a few minutes,' said Jamie. 'Come on, let's go to the fairy house.'

Eldric led the first search party and headed out through the hedge, across the neighbouring field and into Grindlewood Forest. Timber waited patiently with the second group as the children prepared to draw the magic circle.

'We have no idea what this will be like,' said Luke.

'Everyone stay close and hold an animal,' said Jamie.

Oberon tooted. He was sitting on Luke's shoulder.

'Yes, Oberon, you can stay there,' said Luke.

Jemima unpinned the brooch from her collar. She pulled out the pin on the back of the brooch, drew a circle in the grass around the group, then stepped back inside the magical line.

'Ready?' she asked.

'Ready,' they said. Timber howled and Teddy meowed. Oberon gave a final toot-toot as Jemima pulled out the eastern diamond.

'Good luck,' chirped the robins, as the brooch whisked the group away.

What happened next was a complete blur. The children felt themselves float off the ground, shake, spin and swirl, as the whole world whipped around them. For another moment it was all a fuzzy dream, and then they landed with a bump.

'Whoa! That was different,' said Jamie.

'Is everyone OK?' asked Luke. The animals shook their ears, stretched and flexed their paws. Oberon flew to the ground to steady himself.

'I feel a bit wobbly too,' said Abigail, watching the owl fall over a couple of times.

'Hopefully, it'll be easier next time,' said Luke.

'Let's sit down for a minute,' said Abigail.

The four of them sat down, all feeling a bit legless. The animals were already sniffing around. Travelling by brooch obviously didn't bother them too much.

The forest was a beautiful place. Even though it was well into October, the sun was shining, the birds were singing and there was a warm, gentle breeze. The forest floor was thickly carpeted with ferns, dancing bluebells and nodding daffodils – most unusual for the time of year. A fresh fragrance of pine needles filled the air and the children were quickly revived.

'This place is lovely,' said Abigail.

'It's not like other forests at this time of year,' said Jemima in a whisper. 'It's like summer here, not like autumn at all, and it looks so magical.'

'Everything looks magical to you, Jem,' said Jamie, grinning.

'Well, it's not on any normal map, so it really could be anywhere, even another world, couldn't it?' said Abigail.

The others looked at her.

'Like another dimension or a parallel world, or ...' said Luke, but he ran out of ideas.

'I wonder if anyone or anything lives here, other than the birds,' said Jamie after a moment. 'Where are they anyway?'

'They must be at the tops of those incredibly tall trees,' said Luke, lying flat on his back to look straight up. 'I've never seen trees that high before.'

'Come on, let's start looking for the book,' said Jamie.

The group set off. The dogs and Teddy were leaping and bounding through the carpet of flowers. They soon noticed dozens of big butterflies flitting about.

'Look! Rainbow butterflies, just like the ones in Grindlewood,' said Abigail.

'I hope that means the book is here,' said Jamie.

As the children moved deeper into the forest, the trees looked older and even taller than the first ones they saw. The older trunks were immensely wide and straight, with huge, strong branches all reaching upwards towards the sky. They wandered on through more trees and flowers, ferns and bracken, enjoying the walk so much they almost forgot why they were there.

'Hey, where's Timber?' said Jamie suddenly. Timber woofed a few times, but they couldn't see him. They started to panic, realising that they couldn't see Trigger or Teddy either. Up ahead, Oberon was circling around a tree. He tooted loudly and the children ran towards him. The owl disappeared into the tree and flew up inside the trunk. He reappeared higher up.

'Oh, a hollow tree,' said Luke.

'Look over here,' cried Jamie. Timber was at the foot of another tree, half in, half out of the trunk, sniffing furiously for information. Dougal and Teddy were sniffing all around the outside. Some of the scents were strange and unfamiliar. Trigger was charging around in circles, delighted to be able to run around somewhere new.

'Worfeus was definitely here,' said Timber. 'We all recognise his smell.'

'What's that other strange pong?' asked Teddy.

'It could be *The Book of Potions and Spells*,' said Oberon. 'It's bound to smell like other old books. Parchment has a very particular perfume.'

'Is that really perfume?' asked Dougal. He didn't like it much.

'But there's nothing here,' said Timber. 'So where does the scent lead?'

'And what are all those other smells?' asked Trigger.

'They're new to me,' said Dougal. 'The parchment pong only goes all round the tree. Then it stops.'

'The *perfume* is old,' said Oberon. 'The book was probably here some time ago but was moved at some point.'

'Perhaps Worfeus had it in Grindlewood Forest first and then it was brought here,' said Timber.

'But where did it go then?' asked Teddy.

'It might still be here or in Grindlewood Forest, or it could be somewhere else,' said Dougal. 'Oh.'

All they had really discovered were smells.

'We'll have to keep looking,' said Oberon.

The children looked from one animal to the other,

wondering what they were saying.

'Timber, what have you found?' asked Jamie.

His dog looked at him. He made a low rolling growl and then trotted off. Dougal, Trigger and Teddy followed. Oberon flew off to scout further ahead.

'We should follow them,' said Jemima.

'Yep,' said Jamie. 'They might be on to something.'

The search went on for hours. The children walked all over the woods following the animals and the owl. Eventually they became tired, frustrated and hungry.

'This forest is huge,' said Jamie. 'We could be searching for days, even weeks.'

'We should have brought something to eat,' said Luke. 'How did I not think of that?'

'You're right. I'm starving,' said Jemima.

'Me too,' said Abigail, 'and thirsty.'

They sat down in a little clearing.

'What happens if we can't find it?' asked Jemima.

'The queen will keep Timber, that's what'll happen,' said Jamie crossly. He went over to where Timber and Teddy were sitting in the shade. 'Timber's really hot. He needs water. How could I have been so stupid?'

'Where's the owl?' asked Luke. 'He hasn't been around for a while.'

'I don't know. Maybe Timber sent him off somewhere,' said Jamie.

Just then Trigger and Dougal came dashing through the ferns towards the group. Timber barked and looked up. The snowy owl soared in and landed at such speed that he toppled onto Timber's paws.

'Oops! Sorry! I think I may have found it!' he tooted excitedly.

'The book or a stream?' asked Timber.

'Both,' said the owl.

The dogs wagged their tails. Teddy stood up and purred.

'I think Oberon has some good news,' cried Jamie.

The owl tooted to the animals.

'It's about five minutes' flying time – which is a bit of a walk from here. There are more trees, different trees and clumps of trees, but no clear pathway. Then there are five huge oak trees in a clearing. All of them have a wide, deep hole in their trunk, covered by ivy and tiny climbing roses that have lots of sharp thorns. We must take a look, but I didn't want to start pecking before I told you. Anyway, they could be booby-trapped. And there is a stream nearby, so we can all get a drink. Oh, and I saw a very large stag. I'm not sure if he heard me flying about, but he seems to be the only animal around here, other than all of you, of course.' Oberon was so excited, he could hardly stop talking, nor could he stay still.

'Well done,' said Timber.

'This could be it!' said Dougal.

'Trigger, you're the fastest, you run ahead,' said Timber. 'Oberon will lead the way above you. We'll follow with the children.'

Trigger took off straight away, dodging trees, leaping over ferns and crashing through wild flowers as he pelted along. Oberon tooted directions as he soared above the treetops and the children followed with Timber, Dougal and Teddy as quickly as they could.

It took about half an hour for all of them to reach the spot. Oberon and Trigger waited patiently for the others to catch up. The fir trees were very dense just before the clearing, and as the children pushed through the thick branches they stopped dead in their tracks. The animals were standing side by side just ahead of them, staring and growling. Teddy's fur was standing on end. Timber stood in front. A huge stag was blocking their way. He was tall and elegant, with a shiny chestnut coat and towering antlers.

'That is definitely the biggest stag I've ever seen,' whispered Jamie.

'They weren't that big, even in Alaska,' whispered Jemima.

'Let's hope he's friendly,' said Luke.

Then the children got an enormous surprise.

'Good morning, visitors,' said the stag in a deep voice. 'I am Sebastian, guardian of the Eastern Woods. I see you wear Gorlan's ring, young man, but you will not need it today. Tell me, what brings you here? These woods are not on any ordinary map.'

The children were speechless, so Timber approached the stag and spoke for them.

'We are on a quest to find *The Book of Potions and Spells* and return it to its rightful owner, the Forest Queen,' he said.

'And why do you seek it here?' asked the stag.

'The Brooch of Balmedoch brought us to the edge of this forest,' said Timber.

'I see,' said the stag. 'Please, show me the brooch.'

Timber went over to Jemima. He jumped up and pawed at her collar.

'Jem, he wants the brooch,' said Jamie.

'Be careful, we don't know if we can trust the, eh, huge stag,' said Luke. 'Don't let him take it, just show it to him, carefully.'

Jemima took two steps forward and held her collar out.

'It is indeed the enchanted compass,' said Sebastian, 'and the queen would only have given it to those who are worthy. You are welcome.'

Oberon had been sitting on a branch in one of the five oak trees. The stag looked up at him.

'Each tree is enchanted to protect its precious contents, snowy owl. You cannot enter the tree trunk while it is a guardian, nor can you take out what lies within,' said the stag. 'Come and drink from the stream, you all look hot and tired. It will refresh you.'

The three dogs rushed to the stream before the children could stop them. They were desperately thirsty. Jamie walked past the stag and bent down over the water beside Timber. He took a drink and nodded to the others. The water was delicious. The stag was silent while they all drank. With his thirst quenched at last, Timber trotted over to sniff one of the oak trees.

'Which one is the right one?' asked the owl.

'This one,' said Timber, putting his muzzle perilously close to a thick tangle of thorns and curling purple ivy. 'There's very little scent, but somehow I feel it's in this tree.'

'You have a special instinct,' said the stag. 'This is Obadiah Oak Tree,' he said, nodding to the tree. 'He will not give up his treasure easily.'

'But we have to take the book back to the queen,' said Teddy.

'It belongs to her,' said Timber.

'I understand,' said the stag, 'but powerful magic has been used to protect it. Once the Wandelei witch took it back from the warlock, she brought it here and placed it inside Obadiah's trunk for safe keeping. She used a Shield Charm the second time. The first time, someone managed to steal it from one of the younger trees.'

'That could have been Worfeus,' said Timber.

'Or Ripley,' said Teddy.

'Magic is still required to break the spell,' said the stag, 'regardless of who the book belongs to, or who was asked to retrieve it.'

'We really have to do it, Sebastian,' said Jamie. 'We have to take it back to the queen.'

'How can we undo the spell?' asked Jemima.

'Perhaps you have magic of your own?' suggested the stag.

'We can't do magic. We're not witches or wizards,' cried Jamie, instantly regretting what he had said. They looked at Abigail.

'You are like her, little one. You are like the other witch,' said the stag. 'Do you perhaps have magic?'

'I um, I don't know, eh, no,' mumbled Abigail, as she blushed bright red.

'Sorry, Abby,' said Jamie. 'I didn't mean it, like, you know …'

'It's OK,' said Abigail in barely a whisper.

'I know!' shrieked Jemima. 'We can use one of the gemstones!'

'Brilliant!' said Jamie.

'Do you think we should?' asked Luke. 'I mean, we were warned about using them wisely.'

'How else will we get the book?' said Jamie.

'Then you do have magic of your own,' said the stag. 'I will leave you to do what you must.' The giant deer trotted over to the edge of the clearing.

'Do what we must,' muttered Jamie. 'That's what the queen said.'

'What do you think, Timber?' asked Teddy.

'Jemima's right. We need to use a gemstone,' said the malamute. 'There is no other way we can take the book out of that tree.'

The animals and Oberon were quickly in agreement, but Luke and Jamie were arguing about it.

'I just didn't think we would use a gemstone so quickly, that's all,' said Luke. 'Coming here sounded like one of the easier tasks. Visiting the Crabbage Crones and then going north to Bodric will be dangerous. That's when we'll really need magic.'

'We won't even get there, if we don't get this book first,' said Jamie. 'And who knows what the queen will do to Timber if we fail right at the start. Let's take a vote. Hands up all in favour of using a gemstone.'

Jamie and Jemima put their hands up straight away. Abigail was hardly listening. She followed the stag to where he stood by the stream and began gently stroking his neck. She wondered what other secrets her family might not have told her. Even the stag who had never met her before thought she was different.

Timber and Dougal both jumped on Jamie to

say yes. Teddy meowed loudly in agreement. Oberon landed on Luke's shoulder and pecked his ear. Trigger sat at his feet and barked until he gave in.

'I think the owl is telling you what to do,' said Jamie, trying not to laugh, 'and Trigger definitely wants you to agree. Come on, Luke.'

'OK, OK, I give in,' said Luke. 'Don't blame me if we run out of magic later.' He untied the string around his wrist.

'Remember, we have to use them in the right order,' said Jemima. 'The emerald is first, isn't it?'

'That's right,' said Luke, 'the green one.'

He popped the emerald out of its clasp. He took it in his right hand and concentrated hard on thinking only of releasing the Shield Charm on Obadiah Oak Tree. He closed his fist tightly around the stone. He closed his eyes so he wouldn't be distracted. And he wished. He opened his eyes. His hand was empty. They watched the tree, waiting to see what would happen.

After a long, nervous minute, they heard loud groaning and creaking as the spell was slowly reversed. The thorns retreated, and the ivy unravelled, before winding its way higher up the tree. The gap in the trunk yawned wide before them. There, inside, was

The Book of Potions and Spells – the first part of the WABOM.

The noble stag gave a little snort, bowed politely to Abigail and trotted off. Timber barked his thanks and let out a soft howl. When the rest of the group turned to say goodbye, Sebastian Stag was out of sight.

Jamie lifted the book carefully out of the tree trunk. It was large, heavy and looked very old. The brown leather cover was decorated around the edges in gold and the name was written in large letters in dark-green ink.

'The WABOM must be huge when all four parts are together,' said Luke.

'Unless it can do that shrinking thing like *The History of Magic* book,' said Jamie.

'How amazing,' said Abigail. 'A powerful spell book that is centuries old. Can you believe it?'

'I never would have before now,' said Jamie.

'Can we take a look?' asked Jemima.

'Should we?' asked Luke.

'Maybe just a quick look,' said Abigail.

She reached over and gently turned the cover. Inside they saw that same strange witch language again. There were symbols and drawings too, mostly of woodland scenes, plants and wildlife. There was also a lovely drawing of the stag.

'It's beautiful,' said Abigail softly. 'It reminds me of *The Book of Enchantments*, only this book isn't nearly as faded.' She took the little book out of her pocket. Some of the drawings were almost identical.

'Maybe they were both written by the same witches and wizards,' said Jemima.

'Hey, look there, in the middle,' said Luke. 'Some of the pages have been torn out.'

Abigail turned a few pages. 'You're right,' she said. 'I wonder what was on those pages that was so important.'

'And who tore them out?' said Luke.

'I'll bet it was Worfeus,' said Jamie.

'I hope the queen won't think that we took anything,' said Jemima.

'Come on, let's bring it back to her,' said Luke. 'One down, three to go.'

They closed the book gently. Jamie held it tight to his chest. They gathered inside the new circle that Jemima drew in the clearing. When everyone was safely inside, she pushed the eastern diamond back in and the spinning and swirling began again.

Chapter Eleven

FIRST TASK COMPLETE

When the children and pets returned to the garden it was almost dark.

'How long have we been gone?' asked Jamie.

'I didn't think it would be this late,' said Abigail.

'No wonder we're so hungry,' said Jemima.

'My watch has jumped six hours,' said Luke.

'It seems we took longer than we thought,' said Timber to the residents who were waiting for them.

'A lot longer,' said Eldric. 'You've been gone for nearly a day and a half!'

'What!' cried Teddy.

'Isn't it still Sunday?' asked Dougal.

'Nope, it's Monday,' said Ramona. 'Monday evening.'

'Hmm,' said Timber, 'we must be careful

about that. Did you find anything in Grindlewood Forest?'

'We found Worfeus' old lair, a dark and smelly cavern, and his cauldron too,' said Ramona. 'It's covered in moss and it's full of bird and rat bones.'

'We found some crumpled pages with strange writing,' interrupted Eldric. 'They might be the potion recipes that Worfeus used. Take a look.' Eldric pulled back some foliage with his paws. Underneath was a bundle of parchment pages.

'We had to stick them on Norville's spikes to get them all back here,' said Ramona.

'They would have been badly damaged in any of our mouths,' said Eldric. The fox was embarrassed that he hadn't thought of a better idea. The pages were covered with holes from Norville's spines.

'Never mind the holes, it was great that you found them,' said Timber. 'And we found the book.'

'Excellent!' said Eldric.

The birds twittered with delight. The rabbits did a little thumping dance.

'It was hidden in an enchanted tree,' said Timber. 'It's missing a few pages, so hopefully those are the ones you found.'

The children followed the noise to see what was happening. Timber led Jamie to the bushes where the missing pages were stashed. He reached underneath and pulled them out.

'Well done, everyone!' he said to the pets. 'Look what they found,' he said, turning to the others. 'Let's see if they fit.' The children ran back to the fairy house and spread the pages out on the floor.

'They *are* a match!' cried Luke. 'Hey, that wasn't so hard after all!'

'We did it,' said Jamie, looking pleased. 'We all did it.' He rubbed Timber's ears and stroked his head. The dog licked him and trotted outside to tell the others.

'Children, supper's ready!' cried Gloria, coming up from the house.

'Crikey,' said Jamie. 'We'll have to eat quickly and then go to Hollow Hill. I don't think we should wait till the morning.'

'Hello there,' said Gloria, peeping around the doorway. 'I'm glad you two are still here, Luke, Abigail. Why don't you join us for supper? Come on up to the house.'

'Still here?' muttered Luke. 'Eh, thanks very much, Mrs Grindle.'

'Thank you, Mrs Grindle,' said Abigail.

'Come on,' said Jamie, 'this is the fastest supper we'll ever have.'

'Hopefully Mum and Dad are still enchanted,' said Jemima as they ran up to the house.

Luckily, there was no mention during supper of the children having been gone for a day and a half. They were ravenous and gobbled down huge helpings of cottage pie in double-quick time. Then they ran back to the fairy house with Timber in tow.

'There's no need for all the animals to come,' said Jamie. 'The queen only wants to see Timber. Right, boy?' Timber barked. Oberon tooted from the windowsill.

'Maybe the owl wants to come,' said Luke. Oberon tooted, then Trigger barked. 'No Trigger, not this time. You wait here with Dougal. We'll be back soon.'

Timber led the way down the tunnels, with Oberon flying overhead. The butterflies appeared again and flew alongside them. When they reached the chamber, Pendrick was waiting.

'Oh, well done! You did it, well done!' he said, clapping his hands. 'Her Majesty will be pleased. It's wonderful to finally have some good news.'

They hurried to the queen's chamber.

'Ah, Timber,' said the queen, 'and children, welcome. I see you have *The Book of Potions and Spells*. At last, it is back where it belongs. Thank you, thank you.' The queen reached down and took the book. She flicked through it until she came to the torn and missing pages.

'We found the book in the Eastern Woods,' said Luke.

'And the animals and birds found these pages in Grindlewood Forest,' said Jamie. 'We think they're the missing ones from the book.' Jamie handed them to the professor. Pendrick examined them.

'I think you're right,' he said. 'Excellent work!'

'The book can be repaired, can't it, Pendrick?' asked the queen.

'Yes, Your Majesty,' said Pendrick. 'The fairies are very skilled at this kind of thing. They will restore it in no time.'

'Thank goodness.' The queen sounded relieved, but she was keen to press on. 'Your next task is to find *The Book of Light*. Bring it to me tomorrow.'

'Tomorrow?' said Jamie. 'We think we already lost a day today. I mean yesterday … whatever. We left on Sunday morning but came back on Monday evening. Is that right?'

'The first journey is usually the longest,' muttered one of the augurers, as he shuffled past.

'What?' said Jamie.

'Never mind Audmund,' said Pendrick. 'We have tried to correct that problem, but the Wizard Balmedoch had a strange way of doing things.'

'Enough chatter,' said the queen. 'I need the complete WABOM by Halloween.'

'But that's only five more days,' said Luke.

The queen ignored Luke's protest. 'Where in the woods did you find this book?' she asked.

'In a tree called Obadiah,' said Jemima.

'Obadiah is one of five enchanted oak trees,' said the queen. 'You must have used your first gemstone to take it from such a powerful guardian.'

'Yes, we did,' said Luke. 'Did you expect us to use one on the first task?'

'I expect you to choose wisely,' said the queen. 'You have done well on the first task. Go now, and prepare for the next.'

The children walked towards the door.

'Wait,' said the queen. 'Timber is to stay. I want him

to tell me all about your visit to the Eastern Woods, at least until I fall asleep.'

Jamie was furious, but Pendrick shook his head.

'Don't worry,' he said quietly. 'The queen will fall asleep quickly and Timber will follow you home. I promise.'

The queen bent low to pet Timber on the head, then folded her branches and smiled at him, ignoring the children and the owl.

'Come, Timber, tell me the story.'

The big dog sat down beside the tree queen's protruding roots and began the tale in ancient witch tongue. Pendrick walked out slowly with the children. They stopped for a moment in the reception chamber.

'Send Timber home soon,' said Jamie anxiously.

'Of course I will,' said Pendrick. 'Don't worry, the storytelling won't last long. Her Majesty was very anxious today, worn out. She'll need to sleep soon. Good night, then, and good luck tomorrow,' said Pendrick.

'Good night, Professor,' called Luke over his shoulder, and they headed back to Grindlewood. All of them were dragging their feet, hating the fact that they had to leave Timber behind. Jamie was still moping and the others were afraid to speak in case they upset him, when suddenly they heard Timber's big snow paws pad-padding after them.

'Woof!' he barked.

'Hey, good boy, Timber,' said Jamie, giving him a hug.

'Whew,' said Luke. 'I'm glad that didn't last too long.'

They hurried on home in a much better mood.

Early the next morning, Timber came out of the kennel and howled loudly so Trigger could hear him from over on the farm. He had made up his mind about who would be travelling south: Trigger for speed on the ground, and Oberon for eyes in the air.

The residents gathered.

'Today, we are heading south to look for the second part of the WABOM, *The Book of Light*,' said Timber. 'I'd like just a few of us to go this time.'

'Oh?' said Eldric.

'It's just a hunch,' said Timber, 'but I think only Trigger and Oberon should go with us.' He looked around at the disappointed faces. 'A bigger group will be needed to go west and north, but not this time. Teddy, Dougal, keep an eye on things here. You never know who might pop in for a sneaky peek around.'

'OK, Timber,' said Teddy.

'Will do,' said Dougal.

'Eldric, you and your buddies keep an eye out in the forest. Watch for any squirrels and see if you can locate any tunnels. There just might be another entrance to Hollow Hill somewhere in there.'

'Understood,' said Eldric.

'The birds can take turns scouting. Report back to Teddy, OK?'

'Of course we will,' said all the blackbirds in unison. The robins tweeted and the sparrows practised their dives. The heron immediately flew off and took up his lookout post on the roof of the big house. The wood pigeons took their places in the trees and coo-cooed as usual.

'What about us?' asked Serena Swan.

'I was hoping you and Swinford would keep an eye on Lindon Lake,' said Timber. 'Let Teddy know if you spot anything unusual.'

'Right away,' said Serena and off she flew.

'And finally, the rabbits,' said Timber. 'Ramona, I think we're going to need your kick-boxing skills when we go west. Make sure your team is ready for action.'

'No problem,' said Ramona confidently.

All the residents went about their business. Jamie and Jemima came out of the house as their bewitched parents smiled at them from the kitchen window.

'Hi,' said Luke, waving from the side gate. 'Trigger ran ahead of me and got here before I did. He's very excited this morning!'

Jamie opened the gate to let them in.

'He really is so fast and so clever,' said Jemima, petting his ears.

'Timber has organised the animals again,' said Jamie. 'Look!' The other animals and birds were heading off in different directions. Timber trotted over to say hello to Trigger. Oberon toot-tooted and landed on Luke's shoulder. Then Abigail ran out of the house.

'Hi, your mum let me in the front door. Am I late?'

'Hi, Abby. You're OK. Luke has just arrived too,' said Jamie. 'Let's do a check of what we've got.'

'I was going to bring a few scones but they were

still in the oven when I left,' said Abigail. 'Your mum looks really happy this morning.'

'It's the "happy enchantment",' said Jamie. 'I'm not sure if it's funny or annoying.'

'I grabbed a packet of biscuits,' said Luke.

'I took a few bananas,' said Jemima.

'And I've got some water,' said Jamie, 'which is mostly for the dogs. Put everything in my rucksack.'

'Let's check the treasures,' said Luke. They each showed their items in turn.

'Right, I'll draw the circle,' said Jemima. 'This time we're going south. Get ready to spin, everyone.'

They huddled together, the boys holding the dogs. After marking out the circle on the grass, Jemima stepped inside, took a deep breath and pulled out the southern diamond. As the red garnet swirled, the whole world began to spin. This time they saw the moon rushing past them, then the stars, then the sunrise, till they were surrounded by the dawn breaking. They were spinning very fast, then slowing down, then everything went blank.

Chapter Twelve

SHARING SECRETS

It was suddenly bright and very noisy. They could hear familiar sounds before they could see them, and then everything became clear, and then, 'beep-beep', the sound of a horn.

'Hey, we're in Grindlewood village!' said Jamie. 'Watch out!'

They were standing in the middle of the road and had to jump out of the way of a delivery van. Timber and Trigger barked at it as it swerved around them. They hurried to the pavement.

'Is this right?' asked Luke.

'Abigail, we're right outside your house and your granddad's shop!' cried Jemima.

'Oh, that's funny,' said Abigail. 'Why would the brooch take us here? It must be a mistake.'

'Is the compass broken?' asked Luke, looking at it.

'It looks OK,' said Jemima, checking her collar.

'Maybe we should be somewhere nearby, like around the corner or down the road somewhere,' said Jamie.

The children stood together and looked around, wondering where to go.

'Good morning, children! Off on an adventure, are you?'

'Oh, hello, Mrs Emerson,' said Jamie. He looked at Luke as the portly middle-aged lady walked quickly on.

'It's OK,' said Luke. 'Mrs E always says things like that. She always thinks I'm up to something.'

'She often visits Granddad,' said Abigail. 'She spends hours chatting with him and asks lots of questions about everyone and everything.'

'What do we do now?' asked Jemima. 'Should we try the brooch again?'

'Hey, Granddad is calling us in,' said Abigail.

Sure enough, Thaddeus Allnutt was at the window, waving at the children. He went to open the door.

'Come on in, everybody. You too, Timber and Trigger. I've heard all about you. Oh, hello, snowy owl. You're a long way from the tundras of the north. What's your name then?' said Thaddeus, stroking the owl gently on his forehead.

'His name is Oberon, Mr Allnutt,' said Jamie. 'He lives in our barn.'

'What a lovely bird,' said Thaddeus. 'Do come in. I have made some tea in the kitchen. Won't you join me? I can even manage some water for the dogs!'

'Thanks, Mr Allnutt,' said Jemima.

'You're all out early this morning,' said Thaddeus. 'Abigail's mum just went out for some milk. She'll be back shortly. Come along, we have something tasty in the oven.'

They followed Thaddeus through to the back of the house. The nearly baked scones smelled delicious. They sat down around the kitchen table. The dogs sat on the floor and Oberon landed on the windowsill near the Allnutts' nightingale, who was surprisingly pleased to see an owl come to visit.

'So, what brings you to the village at half past eight in the morning?' asked Thaddeus.

'Half past eight?' said Luke. He looked at his watch. The time twist had taken an hour and a half, but they could have walked to the village in ten minutes.

'Em, we were just taking the dogs for a walk,' said Jamie.

'And the owl?' asked Thaddeus, raising his eyebrows, as he peered over his small round glasses that were nearly always perched on the end of his nose. He smiled at them. 'It's all right, Professor Pendrick told me, and I spotted Gorlan's ring and the compass brooch before you even crossed the hallway.'

'You know about the quest and the treasures?' shrieked Jemima, before she could stop herself.

'I most certainly do,' said Thaddeus.

'We found the treasures in our garden a while ago,' said Jamie, 'but we only just found out what they can do.'

'Ah, yes, Wanda must have hidden them in a hurry when she was pursued by Worfeus,' said Thaddeus. 'I'm sure she meant for you to find them, though, in time.'

'Really?' said Jamie. 'But we weren't even living there when she eh, left. Hold on, how do *you* know all this, Mr Allnutt?'

'Because he's a wizard, aren't you, Granddad?' said Abigail, suddenly realising who her grandfather really was. The others sat bolt upright and stared, first at Abigail, then at her granddad. 'That's how you know so much and nothing we've said surprises you. That's how you know the professor and have all these amazing books and all that other stuff in the cellar – all those strange, old things.'

'Yes, dear, you're right. I am a Wandelei wizard, and your mother is a Wandelei witch and Wanda's eldest sister,' said Thaddeus softly.

Abigail just looked at him.

'Your mother and I have a lot to explain, Abigail,' said Thaddeus. 'We were talking about it just the other day. I'm so sorry you had to figure it out by yourself.'

'Wanda was your aunt!' gasped Jemima. 'That's amazing!'

'Gee,' said Luke. 'You do look a bit like her, I mean your aunt, eh, oh!'

'Crikey!' cried Jamie. 'Fantastic! I mean, whoa, more surprises!'

'I'm not surprised about you, Granddad,' said Abigail. 'There were so many things that couldn't be explained. I just never thought that all of our family was magical. Does that include me?'

Abigail's mum had been standing in the doorway. She went into the kitchen and sat beside her daughter.

It was time to explain, and Esther couldn't tell her quickly enough now that the secret was out.

'Abigail, dear, I thought long and hard about this, and I'm sorry I didn't tell you before now. Your father was a brave Wandelei knight who died trying to protect the queen. After that, I took you to live in Grindlewood village, where your granddad joined us later and we opened the antiques shop. We wanted you to be safe and have a normal, happy life away from all those troubles and sad memories.'

Esther hugged Abigail tightly, hoping she would understand.

'Thanks, Mum, and thanks, Granddad,' Abigail whispered, tears falling down her cheeks. 'I wish Dad could be here too, and Aunt Wanda. Did I ever meet her?'

'Only when you were very little,' said Esther.

'They'd be very proud of you, Abigail,' said Thaddeus, 'and glad you are safe and happy and have such good friends.' He smiled at her, hoping she wouldn't be too upset. 'And yes, this means that you could be a Wandelei witch, *if* you learn some magic before your ninth birthday.'

'But that's on Saturday!' cried Abigail. 'This

Saturday is the thirty-first.'

'Yes, dear, your granddad and I have decided to teach you a few spells before your birthday,' said Esther, glancing at Thaddeus. 'After that, you can continue to study magic and become a fully trained witch, if that's what you want.'

'Wow!' said Jemima. 'That's so fantastic!'

'Good for you, Abby!' said Jamie.

Timber and Trigger barked and wagged their tails. Oberon hooted and flew around the kitchen with the nightingale.

'Congratulations,' said Luke, 'and em, sorry about your dad and Wanda.'

Abigail looked around at everyone. She was feeling a little overwhelmed.

'You don't have to decide now, dear,' said Thaddeus. 'The three of us will talk about it later. Right now, we should talk about your next task, finding *The Book of Light*.'

'*The Book of Light*?' said Esther.

Thaddeus adjusted his glasses and looked at Abigail's mother. He expected a bad reaction to the next piece of news. 'Esther,' he said, 'Queen Lyra has asked the children to find the WABOM. Pendrick told me at our meeting late last night.'

'What?' cried Esther. 'Thaddeus, how could she? They're only children.'

'Now, now, settle down,' said Thaddeus. 'They have already found *The Book of Potions and Spells*.' Thaddeus smiled encouragingly.

'Have they? I mean, did you really, children?' said Esther, distracted by Thaddeus' dazzling smile. His enchanted gold tooth came in useful when calm or persuasion were urgently needed.

'Yes, Mum,' said Abigail. 'We found it yesterday in the Eastern Woods.'

'The Eastern Woods! Good heavens!' Esther slumped into a chair.

'They have the queen's treasures too,' said Thaddeus, peering over his glasses again.

'Where on earth …? Oh, of course, the fairy house. Clever Wanda,' said Esther in a whisper. 'But why did the queen choose you?'

'She said we are worthy,' said Jemima.

'And chosen by Wanda, apparently,' said Jamie.

'We managed to get the first book without too much trouble,' said Luke.

'If I'm a Wandelei, does that mean I can't help

now? You know, Wandeleis aren't allowed to take the WABOM, it has to be given back by someone else,' said Abigail.

'Well, as you are not yet a fully trained witch, I think you can be part of the quest, unlike your mother and myself,' said Thaddeus. 'We will, however, be on hand to help you with suggestions and preparations and whatever else we are allowed to do. Won't we Esther?'

'Of course,' said Esther, gulping down some tea. 'Of course we will.'

'The queen threatened to keep Timber if we refused to do it,' said Jamie crossly. 'We didn't really have a choice.'

'I see,' said Thaddeus. 'Never mind her bad moods, Jamie. Pendrick tells me that the queen is not herself any more, but we will do all we can to help you.'

The children chatted quietly as Thaddeus made another pot of tea and Esther took a tray of hot scones out of the oven. She placed them on the table. They smelled absolutely delicious. The children munched hungrily as Thaddeus poured the fresh tea.

'Now children,' he said, 'I want you to tell us everything the queen said about the quest – absolutely everything.'

The children related the whole story about the butterfly message, finding the tunnel, going to Hollow Hill and meeting with the queen and her professors.

'Was this all really started by Wanda?' asked Luke.

'Well, Wanda had a wonderful way of knowing,' said Thaddeus.

'Knowing what?' said Jemima, blobbing jam all over her chin.

'Just knowing,' said Thaddeus, 'knowing who to trust, knowing what to do and when, just knowing. I think she would have been an excellent augurer, if not a queen.'

'Wanda sounds a lot nicer than the present queen,' said Jamie.

'I can see how you might think that,' said Thaddeus, 'but Queen Lyra was the most dedicated and wisest of queens. However, she has spent many years now as a tree and that can't have been easy. It's bound to put her in a bad mood now and again. Did you hear that she must appoint a new queen on Halloween?'

'This Saturday?' asked Abigail.

'Yes, Halloween is a very important day to the Wandeleis,' said Thaddeus. 'Queen Lyra has been queen for fifty years. If she doesn't appoint her successor by Halloween, the augurers will choose someone, and that is not always for the best.'

'Why is that?' asked Abigail.

'Because, my dear, the current augurers don't always agree on everything, even their visions,' said Thaddeus. 'In my opinion, they need to renew their magic more than anyone else and perhaps even find a new augurer or two.'

'I still don't understand why the queen asked *us* to find the WABOM,' said Jamie. 'She asked Wanda to find it first, didn't she?'

'She asked Wanda to do a number of things,' said Esther. 'One of those tasks was to *find out* where the WABOM was. As a Wandelei, she could never have been the one to return it to Hollow Hill.'

'That is one of the first rules of the Ancients,' said Thaddeus. 'The WABOM is a powerful book, but quite strange in its creation.'

'The queen and the professors said something like that, but I thought they were just playing games with us,' said Jamie.

'No, this is no game,' said Thaddeus.

The kitchen was quiet for a moment as they tried to take in what they had heard. Everyone had learned another big secret.

'We found *The Book of Potions and Spells* just yesterday, or was it the day before?' said Luke. 'It was inside a big tree.'

'Ah yes, Obadiah, I'll bet,' said Thaddeus.

'Yes, that's the one,' said Jemima. 'We had to use a gemstone to get it.'

'We took the book to the queen last night,' said Abigail, 'and now she wants us to find *The Book of Light*.'

'And bring it back to her today,' added Jamie.

'Well, I know a bit about *The Book of Light*. In fact, why don't I show you?' said Thaddeus, with a twinkle in his eye.

'Show us?' said Jemima.

'I have lots of things to show you,' said Thaddeus. 'Come along.'

'Are we going to your cellar?' asked Jamie. 'I've been dying to have a look down there.'

'Yes, we are and I'm sure you have,' said Thaddeus. 'Follow me, everyone.'

They went into the hall and down the narrow staircase to the cellar. Thaddeus showed them many strange-looking objects. Some had once been enchanted, he said, but others he wasn't so sure about; others had been famous, like the flying carpet and the genie's bottle. A few items looked quite ordinary, but most of them looked mysterious, old or magical.

'You might like some of these books,' said Thaddeus, handing the children a few tattered novels, 'and I have a good collection on learning magic too – up there, volumes one to one hundred! We'll be starting your lessons with those books, Abigail.'

Abigail said nothing.

'Aren't you excited by all this?' whispered Jemima.

'I'm not sure,' said Abigail. 'I feel like I don't know who I am.'

'It'll take a while to get used to it, dear,' said Esther, 'but you're the same girl you always were and you have an exciting time ahead of you, if you choose it.'

'But I don't know what to choose!' cried Abigail. 'How am I supposed to know what I want?' She raced out of the cellar and up to her bedroom.

'Oh dear,' said Esther. 'What will I do? How can I help her understand?'

'Esther, you know what it's like to be a witch. Tell her about it, reassure her,' said Thaddeus. 'Go on upstairs. I'll join you in a few minutes.'

Esther looked tense as the children watched her leave the room.

Chapter Thirteen

THE BOOK OF LIGHT

While Esther and Abigail were talking, Thaddeus showed the children many of his prized possessions. He was a great collector of unusual things and every item had its own story. After about an hour, he went upstairs to check on Abigail.

The children continued looking around, fascinated by all the mysterious objects. Luke and Jamie were interested in Thaddeus' collection of unusual maps. The embroidered ones were draped across the longest wall. The paper ones were pinned here and there around the rest of the room. There was a collection of globes too, but not all of them were of planet Earth.

The girls were intrigued by an elaborate gold clock. It told the time in many different places, but didn't count time in the way they were used to. There was a fabulously colourful Spanish fan too, which, every time it opened, showed a different picture, sometimes in silk or lace, other times in feathers, sequins or beads.

Oberon was trying to read a book that Thaddeus had left open on one of the bookcases, while Timber and Trigger were happily sniffing every corner of the room. Suddenly, Timber became very interested in a battered old chest that was sitting at the side of Thaddeus' writing desk.

'Trigger, over here, take a sniff at this!' he woofed to his friend. 'I've never smelled anything like this before.'

Jamie noticed the dogs' interest in the chest.

'I'll bet there are lots of funny smells on that old thing,' said Jamie.

'It must have been around the world a hundred times,' said Luke. 'It looks so old. How has it held together all this time?'

'Magic, I suppose,' said Jamie. 'Or maybe it's that rhino-style leather. I doubt if anything could get through that.'

'I wonder what's in it,' said Jemima, looking over. 'Let's take a peek.'

Timber's nose was working very hard to figure out

this chest. He was pawing at it too as if he wanted to get inside. Trigger was running back and forth, getting very excited about it. Oberon fluttered down and landed on the desk to look down on it.

'Yeah, maybe we should take a look,' said Jamie. The boys pulled the chest away from the desk to check the back. It was very heavy and there were scratch marks on the floor where it had been dragged around before.

'Nope, no lock or latch at the back,' said Luke.

They tried to push the lid up from every side but it wouldn't budge.

'There must be a trick to this,' groaned Jamie, straining to lift it again.

'There is,' said Thaddeus. Esther and Abigail followed him into the room.

'Oh, sorry Mr Allnutt,' said Jamie, almost falling over with surprise. 'We were wondering why Timber was so interested in this chest. He wouldn't leave it alone, and then the other two joined in.'

'Is that so?' said Thaddeus. 'Good boy, Timber!'

He went to a drawer in his desk and took out his wand.

'I don't always show this to visitors,' he said, with a twinkle in his eyes. He waved the wand over the chest and mumbled a few words. There was a heavy click and the lid popped open about an inch. Thaddeus flicked his wand to raise the lid a bit higher.

'Wow!' said Luke.

'Cool,' said Jamie.

They peered into the chest, excited at what they might see – but there was nothing. Timber put his front paws on the side of the chest to stand up and then he too looked in. He was still very excited about it even though it looked empty.

'Timber, sit!' said Jamie. 'Sorry, Mr Allnutt.'

'It's all right, Jamie. Your dog has excellent instincts,' said Thaddeus.

'But there's nothing in there,' said Luke.

'Ah, but there is, and Timber knows it,' said Thaddeus.

'More magic,' said Jemima.

'Yes,' said Thaddeus. 'There is a cloaking spell at work and it is a very clever cloaking spell too, even if I say so myself, as I invented it!' Everyone kept staring into the chest, waiting for something to appear. 'It keeps the contents of the chest invisible and almost completely undetectable, unless you are a very gifted magician or have extraordinary instincts, like Timber.'

'What's inside?' asked Jemima.

'It's *The Book of Light*, isn't it?' said Abigail softly.

'Yes, dear, we have *The Book of Light*,' said Thaddeus.

'That is so cool!' said Jamie.

'Terrific!' said Luke.

'How long have you had it?' asked Abigail.

'I was one of the four wizards who were asked to protect the WABOM,' said Thaddeus. 'I have lived in lots of strange places, just so I could keep it safe, but this is where I have kept it for the last seven years.'

'So the brooch took us to the right place after all,' said Jemima.

'Why haven't you taken it back, Granddad?' asked Abigail. 'You were asked to guard it, not find it, so you could take it back at any time.'

'Unfortunately, we can't be sure who we can trust in Hollow Hill,' said Thaddeus.

'You mean there's a traitor?' said Abigail.

'Yes. I've suspected it for some time,' said Thaddeus. 'The professors and I are trying to uncover who it is, so you must promise not to speak to anyone else about it. Understood?'

The children nodded and Timber barked.

'Yes, good boy, Timber,' said Thaddeus. 'The other two parts of the WABOM don't have the same dark and complicated elements that *The Book of Light* and *The Book of Darkness* have. We must be careful with them.'

'Why is that?' asked Jamie.

'It's complicated, Jamie,' said Thaddeus. 'Trust me when I say, that *The Book of Light* contains very powerful magic, rarely used and only by a queen.'

'Oh,' said Jemima.

'That sounds heavy,' said Jamie.

'And what is *The Book of Darkness* for?' asked Luke.

'It contains only dark magic and spells that deal with dangerous things, like punishments, banishment and all the dark arts,' said Thaddeus. 'It was used long ago to banish the Crones to the Crabbage Caves.'

'It takes special skill to master *The Book of Darkness*,' said Esther. 'It is only for advanced magicians.'

'Absolutely,' said Thaddeus. 'With a bit of luck, we will unmask the traitor before all four parts of the WABOM are found and you can return *The Book of Light* safely, and last.'

'What about that squirrel, Ripley?' said Luke. 'None of us liked him much.'

'Timber didn't like him either,' said Jamie. Timber barked to agree.

'Didn't he, indeed? That's interesting,' said Thaddeus. 'Pendrick told me about him, but by the sounds of it, Ripley isn't smart enough to be a traitor all on his own. He may be involved, but I think someone else is behind all this.'

'Granddad, what about all the books you gave me?' said Abigail. 'Were you trying to drop hints or something?'

'Well, I thought you might have a natural interest in magic, and –'

'I thought you said they were storybooks!' cried Esther.

'And they are, Esther! They're stories about magic, and the children love them!'

'I thought they were the best books I've ever read,' said Jemima.

'So did I!' said Abigail.

'I thought they were pretty cool,' said Jamie.

'Me too,' said Luke.

Thaddeus shrugged his shoulders and peered over

his glasses at Esther, as if to say, 'I told you so!'

'Oh my, we had better start your magic lessons right away, Abigail,' said Esther. 'We'll have to find you a wand too.'

'I'd like to use this one,' said Abigail, walking over to a tall cupboard. She took out a small, thin stick from the back of a deep drawer. 'Jemima and I found it near the fairy house. I wasn't sure you'd let me keep it.'

'Let me see it, dear,' said Esther.

'We weren't sure it was a real wand,' said Jemima. 'Is it real?'

'I was hoping it was Wanda's wand,' said Abigail.

Esther took it and looked at it carefully.

'It could be. What do you think, Thaddeus?'

The wizard took the wand and turned it over and over. He smoothed it with his fingers. He smelled it. He used a magnifying glass to look closer. He even shook it and listened to it, though no one heard anything.

'I think it is,' he said softly. 'What a lucky find! But the wand chooses the owner, you know, so keep it, Abigail. If the wand wants to belong to you, then it is yours and no one can take it from you.'

'How exciting!' cried Jemima.

Thaddeus handed the wand to Abigail. She stood there holding it, thinking. Jamie wasn't sure if she was about to burst into tears again, so he changed the subject.

'What will the queen do when we don't bring *The Book of Light* back today?' he asked. 'She'll be expecting it.'

'We'll go with you and explain,' said Esther.

'Yes, let's do that now,' said Thaddeus. 'I'm sure she'll understand once I tell her she has a traitor in her midst. Now follow me, everyone, we have a tunnel to Hollow Hill in this house too, you know!'

Thaddeus rolled back the Persian rug in the middle of the stone floor. He opened a trap door, which revealed big limestone steps twisting down to another cellar below. The lower cellar led to a tunnel, which connected to the main tunnel to Hollow Hill.

'We received a message the other day, to say that the tunnels were open again,' said Thaddeus. 'I knew then something big was about to happen. Now, down you go, children, dogs and owl. Esther and I will be right behind you.'

Chapter Fourteen

TRAITORS ON THE LOOSE

'Wait here,' said Thaddeus when they arrived at the reception chamber. 'Pendrick and I will talk to the queen first. We shouldn't be long.'

Thaddeus headed down the narrower tunnel towards the queen's chamber. He found Professor Pendrick, who was looking rather troubled.

'Her Majesty is not in good form,' he said. 'Hopefully her mood will improve when she hears we have *The Book of Light*, or rather you have it.'

Thaddeus frowned. 'Let's hope so, because we also have some bad news.'

Pendrick entered the chamber first. The queen was just recovering from another bout of wailing.

'Have the children returned with Tyrus?' she asked.

'Ahem, it's Timber, Your Majesty,' said Pendrick,

bowing. 'They will be along shortly, but there is someone else who wishes to see you first.'

'Yes, yes, who is it?'

'Thaddeus Allnutt, Your Majesty,' said Pendrick, waving Thaddeus in.

'Allnutt!' cried the queen. 'The Wizard Allnutt? Where have you been? Weren't you given charge of *The Book of Light*?'

'Yes, Your Majesty, and it is safe,' said Thaddeus, bowing to the queen.

'Thank goodness. We didn't know if you were alive or dead,' said the queen. 'Pendrick, you could have told me!'

'I heard from the Wizard Allnutt only the other day, Your Majesty,' said Pendrick. 'Until then, I didn't know for certain where he was or where the book was.'

'I see,' said the queen, unconvinced. 'I remember now – your son Edward was one of my knights. It was a tragedy that we lost him.'

'Thank you, Your Majesty. His widow, Esther, lives with me in Grindlewood.'

The queen muttered Esther's name a few times, trying to recall.

'Your Majesty, I know of the quest to find the WABOM,' said Thaddeus. 'I know these children. In fact, I was speaking with them earlier today.'

'Oh, so they *do* have *The Book of Light*,' said the queen.

'Not quite, Your Majesty, I instructed them to leave it where it is – in my safe keeping,' said Thaddeus. 'When the other parts of the WABOM have been found, they will bring it to you.'

'Why on earth should it stay where it is?' cried the queen. 'I want my book back now!'

'Your Majesty, the Wizard Allnutt and I believe there is a traitor in Hollow Hill,' said Pendrick.

'What? Impossible! It can't be true.'

'I'm afraid it is, Your Majesty,' said Thaddeus. 'In fact, we believe there may be more than one.'

'Outrageous! Who are they?'

'We are still gathering evidence, Your Majesty, but please be careful about confiding in anyone, including your close companions,' said Thaddeus.

'You mean my fairies and my squirrel? Unbelievable!' cried the queen. 'How can you be sure?'

'Well, we aren't sure, Your Majesty,' said Pendrick, 'but …'

'But the risk of losing one of the most important parts of the WABOM – yet again – is simply too great,' said Thaddeus, more firmly.

'The squirrel is a flighty creature,' said Pendrick, 'and there are rumours –'

'Rumours, what rumours? Ripley likes to wander about. He is probably bored sitting here with me,' said the queen.

'Your Majesty, please trust us,' said Thaddeus. 'Your professors are learned men and they have long suspected someone to be leaking information from your royal palace, and now from Hollow Hill. Please do not confide in Ripley or anyone but the professors and myself. We will expose the traitors as soon as possible.'

'They must be after the WABOM,' said the queen after a moment. 'They know of our need to renew our magic and how important it is to have it back before Halloween.'

'Very likely, Your Majesty,' said Pendrick.

'I am only too aware of the urgency to find the WABOM, Your Majesty,' said Thaddeus. 'One of the children on this quest is my granddaughter, Abigail.'

'Ah,' said the queen. 'I knew there was something

about her. Why didn't my augurers mention it. And why didn't they tell me about these traitors? They are taking a long time to do anything these days.'

'Indeed,' said Pendrick, rolling his eyes. 'Shall I go and see how they are getting on?'

'In a moment, Pendrick. I want to see the children and Tyrus now, please,' said the queen.

'It's Timber, Your Majesty,' said Pendrick. 'They are waiting in the reception chamber. I will fetch them now.'

The children, Timber, Trigger and Oberon entered the queen's chamber. Thaddeus, Esther and the professors stood alongside them. The queen spoke to Esther first.

'Esther, welcome, it has been a long time,' said the queen.

'Yes, seven years, Your Majesty. Allnutt is my married name, but I am of the Willow family.'

'Ah yes, the seven Willows,' whispered the queen. 'I remember now. You are one of Wanda's sisters.'

'The eldest, Your Majesty, Wanda was the youngest,' said Esther. 'There were seven of us, but only two remain – Tamara and I.'

'How sad. Where is your sister now?'

'She lives in Grindlewood village,' said Esther. 'Her husband was also killed by the Worfagons.'

'Your family has suffered a great deal,' said the queen softly. 'Thank you for returning, Esther. Tell Tamara we would be very happy to see her return too.'

'I will, Your Majesty. Thank you,' said Esther.

'Everyone, please sit.'

The queen waved a branch with a wrinkled leaf-hand. Plump cushions and low tables appeared, neatly laid with napkins, plates, cutlery and glasses. The queen spoke to the children.

'I believe you have found *The Book of Light*, but the Wizard Allnutt wishes it to remain hidden.'

'That's right,' said Jamie.

'And I agree,' said the queen, 'but you will bring it to me as soon as you recover the other books. Do I make myself clear?'

The children nodded and Thaddeus bowed.

'Today, we should mark the return of the Wizard Allnutt and Esther, and the imminent return of *The Book of Light*.' She waved her wand again and food and drink appeared on the tables. As everyone filled their plates and sat down on the cushions to chat, the queen called Timber to her.

'Come, Timber, son of Tyrus, tell me of today's adventures.'

Jamie nearly choked on his sandwich as he watched Timber trot over to the queen. The malamute sat down on a thick pile of fallen leaves. The children heard him growl and bark softly to her in witch language. He was now more fluent than Oberon.

'Keep cool, Jamie,' said Luke under his breath. 'She's not hurting him, she's just listening to him.'

'I know, I know,' said Jamie, 'but she treats him like he belongs to her. And what's this "son of Tyrus" business?'

Thaddeus leaned over. 'Luke's right, Jamie, stay calm,' he said. 'We don't want to upset Her Majesty, trust me.'

Jamie let out a heavy sigh and stuffed a few more sandwiches in his mouth. The fuller his mouth, the less he would be able to argue.

They all tucked into a lovely spread of sandwiches, cakes, pies and ice cream, washed down with very strange-looking but delicious lemonade.

'Mmm, this must be witch cordial,' said Jemima. 'I love the orange, lemon and green bits in it.'

'It's fairy lemonade,' said Lotus, as she walked past. 'I'm glad you like it. I made it myself.'

'It's delicious,' said Abigail. 'Thank you.'

'You're welcome,' said Lotus. She smiled warmly at Abigail as she went to attend to the queen. Timber had finished telling her of the day's events, not that much had happened, or rather, he didn't tell her much. He reckoned Thaddeus might like to keep the invisibility chest a secret a little longer, and he couldn't be sure who else might be listening. The queen rested her head on a branch and Timber trotted back to the children.

'You see? The queen is drifting off to sleep,' whispered Pendrick. 'Well done, Timber. You helped her to relax.' Pendrick rubbed the dog's ears and received a generous lick in return.

'Great, can we go now?' asked Jamie.

'I think we should,' said Thaddeus. 'There's nothing more to be done here today.'

They got up and left the chamber quietly, careful not to wake the sleeping queen.

'You won't need the brooch to get home tonight,' said Thaddeus. 'We can take the tunnels.'

'Just push the diamond in,' said Pendrick. 'That

will close the portal to the south. Good luck with the third task everyone.'

'Did he say portal again?' asked Luke as they walked out.

'Of course, what else would it be?' said Jemima.

'So we went through a portal. Sure, why not?' muttered Jamie, trying to convince himself that travelling through a portal was not unusual now.

Abigail noticed the worried look on her mother's face and guessed what she was thinking.

'Don't worry, Mum, we can do it,' she said.

'And anyway, we don't have a choice, Mrs Allnutt,' said Jamie quickly. 'We told you what'll happen to Timber if we don't finish the quest.'

'I understand, dear,' said Esther. She moved a bit closer to her father-in-law. 'Thaddeus, they can't go after *The Book of Wisdom*. They can't! Haven't they done enough already?'

'Let's talk about it at home, Esther.' Thaddeus changed the subject and told a few funny stories as they walked down the tunnels together. When they were about halfway back to Grindlewood, they stopped briefly before heading down the two tunnels for home, one to the village and one to the fairy house.

'Children, come and see me tomorrow at about eleven,' said Thaddeus. 'I'll have a few tips for the next task, and Abigail might have learned a spell or two by then.'

'OK, Mr Allnutt,' said Luke.

'Ooooh, best of luck with the magic lessons, Abigail!' said Jemima, giving her friend a hug.

'Good luck, Abby,' said Jamie. 'You never know, your spells might come in handy.'

Back in the queen's chamber, the professors looked on anxiously as the queen's branches thrashed from side to side.

'Another nightmare,' said Flint.

'It's a bad one,' said Sparks.

Audmund glanced at them from under his hood as he walked across the chamber and then disappeared down a side tunnel.

'He's in and out of the chamber a lot lately,' said Flint.

'Let's hope those augurers don't have a say in who the next queen will be,' said Pendrick.

'The queen's nightmares are becoming more

frequent,' said Sparks. 'I hope she won't descend into madness. If she does, her choice might be rather a strange one.'

'We must hope that our new Grindlewood Army will succeed,' said Pendrick. 'That's all that can save us now. We are halfway there, gentlemen – two books recovered and two still to find.'

Chapter Fifteen

PREPARING FOR WEST

With only four days to go until Abigail's ninth birthday, the lessons in magic began in earnest. The Allnutts were up early and all three of them were very excited. They had had another family chat before bedtime and Abigail was feeling more relaxed about becoming a Wandelei witch. Thaddeus had worked late into the night preparing her first lesson from his collection of books about learning magic. With a quick flick of his wand, two beautiful books flew off the shelves and landed on his desk.

'I will be teaching you all about magic, Abigail — theory, history and responsibility,' said her granddad.

'And I will be showing you how to use your wand and cast a few simple spells to begin with,' said Esther. 'We will be adding to your magic skills as you master each lesson and each spell.'

'What if I'm no good at magic?' asked Abigail.

'We were all rubbish at this when we started,' said her granddad, smiling. 'It takes lots of practice to get it right, but you'll get the hang of it, you'll see.'

'You'll do just fine,' said Esther. 'Now, put on your coat and we'll go out to the garage. It's the best place to do lesson one.'

'Have fun, girls!' called Thaddeus.

There was a lot of banging and crashing as Abigail became accustomed to using a wand. The noise would later be described as 'decluttering the garage' to any inquisitive neighbours.

Luke had called in very early to see Jamie and Jemima.

'Hello, Luke. You're just in time for breakfast,' said Gloria as she opened the front door. 'I have a huge pot of porridge ready.'

'Thanks, Mrs Grindle,' said Luke.

'Hello, Luke, hello, Trigger,' said Greg. 'Another early walkies, is it?'

'Hello, Mr Grindle. Yes, I'll just let Trigger outside,' said Luke, eyeing Jamie and Jemima, who were at the breakfast table.

'We have to go to the Allnutts' house now!' whispered Luke, as urgently as he dared. Greg and Gloria had started to read the morning newspapers and didn't look up.

'Mr Allnutt said to call over at eleven,' said Jemima.

'But we have to use the brooch to travel west at seven o'clock, remember? It's ten minutes to seven right now,' whispered Luke in a panic.

'Then why did Mr Allnutt say to call in at eleven?' whispered Jamie. 'He must have known we wouldn't be able to go until tomorrow if we missed the deadline. I hope the queen won't be raging.'

'You can stop whispering,' said Jemima. 'The butterflies flew in while we were feeding the pets. They've already landed on Mum and Dad's hair.'

'Oh, good, fine,' said Luke.

'We can't leave now anyway. Mr Allnutt wants to help us prepare,' said Jemima, 'and Abigail is having her first lesson in ma …'

'What's Abigail doing today?' asked Gloria, peeping over her newspaper.

'What? Um …'

'We're calling in after breakfast,' said Luke.

'You must have a very busy day planned, starting so

early. How nice to have a fun-filled mid-term break!' said Gloria. She smiled at them then returned to her newspaper.

After gulping down their porridge, the children pulled on their coats, hats and scarves and raced out the back door. Timber barked a few times and then trotted past the kennel to the little orchard. Trigger followed, then Dougal and the cats. The other residents were waiting for them.

'Oh, what is all the racket,' said the Brigadier, waking up slowly. 'Why are you all so energetic so early? Oh, hello Trigger. What's happening today, then?' He trundled after the other dogs.

'We're not going after *The Book of Wisdom* until tomorrow,' said Timber.

'Aw, really?' said the sparrows.

'What's the delay?' asked Ramona.

'Mr Allnutt wants to talk to the children first,' said Timber, 'and Abigail is having wand lessons.'

'It's just gone seven by my reckoning,' said Norville. 'That means we've lost another day, and who knows how long it is in magic time.'

'I know time is tight,' said Timber, 'but we need all

the help and advice we can get. The queen told me that the Crabbage Caves are a prison. The crones are a nasty bunch.'

'It's going to be much more dangerous this time,' said Oberon.

Everyone quietened down.

'How many of us are going west?' asked Dougal.

'Almost everyone,' said Timber.

'I suppose we should stay,' said Serena Swan.

'Thank you, Serena,' said Timber. 'I think it's best that you, Norville, the robins and wood pigeons should remain here.'

The birds nodded. Norville didn't protest either.

'Let's talk again when we return from the Allnutts',' said Timber, and he trotted back to the house.

'Come in, come in,' said Thaddeus. 'We have a lot to talk about today.' There were a few more bangs and pops out the back. 'Don't worry about the noise. Abigail is doing splendidly!'

'Um, won't the queen be annoyed if we don't turn up today?' asked Jamie. 'She'll want to see Timber and I don't want to annoy her.'

'I've already sent our nightingale to Hollow Hill with a message, but we'll pop in for a short visit later,' said Thaddeus. 'I'll explain that I was instructing you for tomorrow. She'll understand.' Jamie looked anxious as he stroked Timber's head. 'Don't worry, Jamie,' said Thaddeus. 'The queen looks and sounds meaner than she really is. All will be well.'

There was a massive bang in the back yard.

'Ah, that'll mean break time,' said Thaddeus. 'Abigail is making good progress.'

The children weren't so sure. It sounded like the garage was blowing up over and over again. When teacher and pupil finally came in, Abigail was beaming.

'Hi, everyone,' she said. 'This is such fun! I think I finally got one spell right and another one nearly right, but it isn't nearly as easy as it looks or sounds.'

'It didn't sound very easy,' said Luke, making a face.

'Well done, Abby,' said Jamie. He nudged Luke.

'Yes, super!' said Luke.

'I wish I could try it!' cried Jemima.

'I'm very proud of how Abigail is doing, but this is serious,' said Esther. 'You must be very careful in the west. Pay close attention to what Thaddeus is going to tell you now.'

'Gather round, everyone,' said Thaddeus. The children sat down around the kitchen table. 'Now, the Crabbage Crones are outlaws, criminals. They were imprisoned in the caves for misusing their magic and will remain there until the end of their days. They live beside a rocky seashore that is thickly covered with a particularly smelly seaweed. Do not touch it! It is poisonous. Do not go near the sea! It is full of demons from the deep, extraordinary creatures but deadly in every way.'

'Really, Granddad?' said Abigail. The others were wondering if he was exaggerating too.

'I'm afraid so, dear,' said Thaddeus.

The golden eagle and the kestrel flew towards the setting sun. There weren't many who knew the way to the Crabbage Caves, but Gildevard had superb navigation skills, as well as having Bodric's cryptic clues. He had unravelled the puzzle quickly and so far the directions had been surprisingly accurate.

Gildevard and Kelvin arrived in good time to see the crones prepare steaming potions in several large cauldrons dotted around the beach – just out of reach of the poisonous seaweed and the roaring waves. They were always excited by a full moon, and would celebrate it that night by drinking gallons of specially prepared brews.

They lived in a maze of caves on the western seaboard, somewhere not on any normal map. It was an enclosed place, set between worlds; not part of the human world, not part of the magical world, perhaps in another dimension – no one was sure. All of them looked wizened, and some were indeed very old. Every one of them was nasty. They were always arguing and fighting with each other as they had little else to do except fly around on broomsticks, but they could never fly away.

Some crones were one-eyed, their single bulging eye sticking out of the centre of their forehead. Others were frightfully ugly, covered in boils and carbuncles. Two of the crones had three eyes, but they didn't all have sight. All of them were dirty, ragged, stooped and small, and very, very cunning.

Gildevard and Kelvin swooped smoothly down to land. From a safe distance they watched witches stir the cauldrons, while others fought over scraps or bones. Suddenly, the crones cackled with excitement. The brew was ready. They swarmed in from all directions, squabbling and pushing to get to the pots of potion first, eager to slurp down as much jolly-juice as they could.

'Good,' said Gildevard. 'The crones will fall into a deep sleep once they drink enough juice.'

'It doesn't affect all of them the same way, though, does it?' said Kelvin.

'That's true,' replied the eagle, 'but we won't need long to look for the book. I know exactly where it is.'

'Bodric told you?' said Kelvin.

'He gave me clues,' said Gildevard.

'But how will we carry it, master? Isn't it heavy and awkward?'

'I can manage,' said Gildevard.

In fact the eagle wasn't sure how they would carry it, but his eagerness to get it was causing him to ignore this problem.

The biggest cauldron sat on a smouldering fire on the sand. It was spewing out dark-green smoke into the late-afternoon sky.

'Dinner doesn't smell too inviting,' cackled one crone.

'No, it's another bucket of slop!' grumbled another.

'But that jolly-juice is the best we've ever made,' said a third. 'It'll make up for the lack of decent grub.'

'Who knows what fool might pay us a visit and end up in the pot!'

They all roared laughing.

It was another hour before the crones had guzzled enough to finally doze off, most of them around the fire. Others collapsed here and there on the rocks. Some retreated back to the caves.

'Now is our chance,' said Gildevard. 'We must be quick. Follow me to the cave where they keep the book and wait at the entrance. Hoot if there's trouble.'

Kelvin nodded.

The two birds flew in a high arc. They dived straight down to the entrance of the cave, turning tightly as they flew inside, hugging the cave wall. Luckily, Gildevard had a super radar because there was an extraordinary honeycomb of caves. They reached the innermost part and, sure enough, there was the book, lying on a square stone table.

Kelvin waited at the entrance. Gildevard went inside. The eagle lifted the book with his large, strong talons but it was much, much heavier than he expected. Kelvin had been right about that. How had *he* known? Gildevard pushed the thought out of his mind and looked carefully at his prize. He couldn't leave without it, not now. He tried again. This time he managed to clasp it, but then he dropped it and it slid off the stone table and onto the ground.

'Kelvin, come at once. I need your help,' called the eagle.

But instead of flying to Gildevard's aid, the crafty kestrel flew out to warn the crones.

'You have an intruder. Quick! In the caves!' he squawked and hid amongst the rocks.

The eagle couldn't believe his ears. 'That no-good, deceitful wretch! How could he do this to me?'

Gildevard tried again to lift up the book. He hooked it with his great talons and struggled to fly to the outer cave. His wings were aching. His talons were losing their grip. Then he dropped the book in shock. A wall of crones on broomsticks was blocking the exit. They hadn't drunk too much jolly-juice after all.

❧

It was a long and busy day listening to Thaddeus' instructions, and the children were tired out.

'That's enough for today,' said Thaddeus, shutting his books. 'It's time for some chocolate cake and lemonade, and water for the dogs, of course. Then we shall pay a quick visit to the queen. Come along.'

After finishing a plate of Esther's berry scones *and* a big chocolate cake, they went to the cellar. Thaddeus lifted the Persian rug, unlocked the trapdoor, and everyone climbed down the stone steps into the lower cellar. Timber led the way to Hollow Hill, his tail swishing cheerfully. But Jamie wasn't cheerful. He felt uneasy every time they visited the queen. When they reached the chamber, he took a deep breath.

'It'll be OK, Jamie,' said Abigail, noticing how tense he was. 'Granddad knows what to say.'

'We've been preparing for our next task, so she can't be cross,' said Jemima.

'Here comes Pendrick,' said Luke.

They went into the queen's chamber and Thaddeus explained their plans, but the queen was very irritable.

'This is intolerable!' she roared. 'Haven't I waited long enough? I thought you were here to deliver the book to me. Get me my WABOM or I will punish you, all of you! Timber will stay here with me tonight. You can collect him tomorrow before you go west – to make sure you go west!'

'What? No way!' cried Jamie. 'Timber has to come home. He, he has to be fed. And, and how will I explain it? And, and … you can't keep him here! You can't!' Jamie was livid. Timber was howling and Trigger was barking too.

The queen swished her branches at them. 'Go! NOW!' she roared.

The three professors ushered everyone out of the chamber, except Timber.

'What'll she do to him?' said Jamie. He was shaking with rage.

'Nothing,' said Thaddeus. 'She just wants some company, that's all, right Pendrick?'

'Of course.'

'He will be well fed and watered,' said Flint. 'I'll make sure of it.'

'This is just awful,' said Esther. 'I'm so sorry this has happened, Jamie, everyone.'

'It's no one's fault, Esther,' said Thaddeus.

'I feel like it's my fault. If only I had prepared Abigail sooner.'

'Nonsense,' said Thaddeus. 'That has nothing to do with the queen's bad mood. She will calm down. All will be well.'

'Timber will be waiting for you in the morning,' said Pendrick. 'Come early, so you can return to Grindlewood to take the other residents with you to the west.'

'How did you know we would be taking the others?' asked Luke.

'You're going to need them,' muttered Audmund as he slunk past.

'Ignore Audmund,' said Pendrick. 'I'm sure Timber will have asked some of his garden friends to help. He understands all of this more than you know. Now, go home and try to relax for the evening. Tomorrow is a very big day.'

Chapter Sixteen

THE CRABBAGE CRONES

It was still dark when Jamie got up and dressed. He rushed downstairs and out the kitchen door to the yard. Luke was waiting for him at the side gate. He had arrived even earlier.

'Pssst, Jamie!'

'I'm glad you're here. I couldn't sleep,' said Jamie as he let Luke in. Trigger was with him, wagging his tail furiously.

'Hey, I think this might be Abigail,' said Luke, turning around. Abigail's granddad pulled the car in close to the side gate. He gave his granddaughter a hug.

'Good luck, dear. Try to remember your spells.'

'Thanks, Granddad, I will,' said Abigail.

Thaddeus watched her run over to the boys. He

hadn't felt so worried in a long time.

'Hey, wait for me,' cried Jemima, as she burst out the kitchen door.

'Shhh! You'll wake Mum and Dad,' said Jamie.

'I didn't hear a sound from them,' said Jemima. 'Hi, Luke. Hi, Abigail. Great, we're all here.'

They looked nervously at each other.

'Have we got everything?' asked Jamie.

'I have my own bow and lots of arrows, yours and mine,' said Luke, holding them up, 'and the string of stones,' he added, showing his wrist.

'I've got the ring and my wooden sword,' said Jamie.

'Jemima has the brooch and Abigail has her wand. Yep, that's the lot,' said Luke.

'All set then,' said Jamie. 'Now, let's get Timber back.'

The children ran into the fairy house, opened the trap door and climbed down the ladder to the tunnel below. The Grindlewood butterflies had been waiting by the well and they followed them down. They flew beside them all the way to Hollow Hill.

Having run most of the way through the tunnels, the children arrived panting. They stood to catch their breath in the reception chamber, but Jamie kept walking quickly.

'Shouldn't we wait for Pendrick?' said Luke.

'No!' said Jamie. 'I want to find Timber and we don't want to run out of time.'

The others hurried after him across the first chamber, down the smaller tunnel, then the next one and then they stopped. The door was open and they could see Timber sitting at the foot of the huge tree. He jumped up and ran over to Jamie, wagging his tail. The queen opened her eyes slowly and stretched her branches. More dead leaves fell from her boughs making her look gaunt and even sadder.

'Follow Timber's lead, children,' she said. 'I have given him good advice.'

'Mr Allnutt gave us advice too,' said Jamie.

'Good,' said the queen. 'I look forward to seeing you later – with *The Book of Wisdom*.'

Then Timber did a strange thing. He turned back to the queen and licked her last hanging leaf-hands.

'Come on, Timber,' said Jamie, scowling as he grabbed his dog by Cordelia's Collar.

'Don't upset her, Jamie,' said Luke through his teeth. 'We've got Timber back, now let's just go.'

Trigger said hello to Timber with a few sniffs and then the two dogs bounded out of the chamber with the children. When they emerged in the fairy house, Timber and Trigger ran quickly out to the waiting residents.

'OK everyone, I need all the dogs, cats and Eldric,' said Timber.

They all moved into a line, side by side.

'Ramona, have you got a team ready?'

'I certainly do!' she replied as three large brown rabbits appeared out of the hedge.

'Good, then you can come too,' said Timber. 'Sparrows, blackbirds, Cyril, I must tell you that this task could be very dangerous. Are you still sure you want to come?'

'That's what our stunning beaks are for!' cried the sparrows.

'We're sure!' cried the blackbirds.

Cyril squawked and flapped his wings.

'All right then, let's go.'

They joined the children and Oberon, who were waiting on the lawn. Abigail picked up Ramona and held her tightly. The other three rabbits huddled at her feet. Jemima held the two cats, Teddy and Cindy, one under each arm. The dogs and the fox stood patiently, ready for action.

Jamie took the brooch from his sister's coat collar and pulled out the pin at the back. He drew the magic circle on the grass, making sure it was big enough to fit everyone. He stepped inside the magical line and pulled out the western diamond.

'Off we go weeeesssst,' cried Eldric, as the world spun and swirled and the brooch took them to a dangerous prison, a place not on any normal map.

They arrived with a thump and everyone fell over. The birds were all a flutter and the animals shook their ears madly.

'Another bumpy one!' cried Jamie.

'And noisy too,' said Luke, rubbing his ears.

'It's the afternoon already,' said Abigail.

'Why did it take so long to get here?' said Jemima.

'We have to get out of here before seven o'clock, otherwise we'll be stuck here till tomorrow morning,' said Jamie.

'We definitely don't want that,' said Jemima.

'Let's draw the circle now, so it's ready for us to leave,' said Luke. 'Jemima, I'll put the brooch in my jacket pocket. It has a zip so it'll be safer there, OK?'

'Good idea,' said Jemima, handing him the brooch. Luke drew the circle and then put the brooch in his pocket.

'Here's a little map of the caves,' said Abigail.

'Where did you get that?' asked Jamie.

'Granddad drew it last night.'

'That's great!' said Jamie. Timber barked and prodded the map with his nose. 'You like the map, Timber? Good boy.' Timber put his paw on it.

'I think he knows something,' said Jemima.

'Maybe the queen told him something about the caves,' said Luke.

Timber growled softly.

'Maybe she did,' muttered Jamie.

'Listen,' said Abigail. 'I can hear the waves.'

'That means we're close,' said Jamie. 'Let's go.'

The children walked a little way, and then ducked down behind some sand dunes. They peeped up behind the scrubby grass that grew along the tops of the dunes. Several crones were down on the beach. The biggest cauldron was bubbling and there were lots of empty potion bottles and pots strewn about. There were so many crones on the beach, they wouldn't be able to reach the caves just yet. A sharp wind was blowing in off the sea, bringing the smells right up to where the children were crouching.

'Ugh!' said Jemima. 'What a pong!'

'It must be that deadly seaweed,' said Luke. 'Remember, don't go near it.'

'This whole place looks weird and smells weird,' said Jamie. 'The water is a funny brown colour and the waves don't all run onto the shore. Look! Some of them go sideways, and then get sucked down under the surface.'

'That must be the demons of the deep,' said Abigail. 'That sea really does swallow things.'

'I never want to see this place a second time,' said Jemima, wrinkling her face again. 'Let's get the book as quickly as we can.'

Timber growled. The animals and birds spread out across the dunes. They noticed another smell – the crones.

'My goodness, they smell very bad,' said the owl. 'And what sort of foul broth is being cooked in that pot?'

Suddenly, there was a lot of commotion. The dogs started barking. The cats hissed. Oberon screeched.

'Look out!' barked Timber, as two crones flew overhead on broomsticks. They zoomed past again, and then flew back to the others who were lounging on the sand. The scouts had been quick to spot the visitors.

'Last night's supper might have left us hungry, but we'll have a fine one tonight!' cried one of them as she flew over the beach.

'Get them!' cried another. A dozen crones leapt onto broomsticks that were lying nearby. They whizzed over to where the children and animals were desperately trying to hide in the sand dunes and rocks. It was already too late. The scouting crones were back, whooshing back and forth above them, and then they began casting spells.

All of the birds took to the sky and swooped and swerved in amongst the crones, trying to surprise them, hoping to knock them off their broomsticks. The other crones scurried across the beach to see what was going on. Timber barked orders to the animals: 'Trigger, stay with Luke.' Trigger barked back and scurried around Luke, who was preparing his bow and arrows. 'Teddy and Eldric, stay with Jemima. Cindy, Ramona and rabbits, you're with Abigail. Make sure

those crones don't get her wand. The queen said it's very important. Dougal, stay close to Jamie.' Timber jumped on Jamie and pawed at his sword. Then he turned and headed towards the caves.

'Timber, no!' cried Jamie, but his dog didn't turn back. The queen had told him how to find the book and he had to get to it quickly.

The children had planned that the boys would use their weapons to fend off the crones while the girls would try to reach the caves, but they hadn't expected quite so many crones. Abigail and Jemima were edging their way up the rocks, trying to see where Timber had gone. He looked like he knew where to go, and they had a map, but they couldn't be sure they would find the book, or if it would be guarded when they did.

The Grindlewood birds were attacking the crones in the air and the animals were fighting others on the ground. Luke had become a good archer over the summer. He was firing off arrows very quickly and many were hitting their targets. Just like in the garden, when they had fought evil before, a dead crone turned to dust. Trigger darted about collecting the spent arrows for Luke, as he quickly reloaded and fired them off again and again.

The gold cross shone brightly in the centre of Gorlan's ring. Jamie held the sword up in front of his face and watched the wooden toy turn into the shiniest, strongest steel. It felt light in his hands yet he knew it was powerful. A few crones screeched when they saw it, and they turned and fled. Jamie suddenly felt inspired.

'I want that book and I want my dog back! Aaaaaaaahh!' he cried, charging forward. He went straight at the crones, first to chop their wands in half and then he went after the crones themselves. The smaller ones transformed into weird looking bats and tried to fly out of reach. Jamie swished and slashed with his sword again and again, cutting them down before they could get away.

It wasn't all going smoothly, however. Several animals were injured as dozens more crones appeared from behind the rocks and even more flew out on broomsticks from the lower caves. Most of them were firing spells as they flew. The cats, the fox and the rabbits all had injuries as they tried to protect the children from getting hit.

Abigail looked behind and below her. Trigger and

Dougal had been hit again and both were limping and whining. 'Jemima, I have to help them!' she cried. 'You go on up. It's time I tried my spells. Here, take the map. Find Timber and the book.'

Jemima looked back for a moment. Teddy was hobbling after her. Eldric had stopped further back. He couldn't walk at all. She grabbed the map from Abigail's outstretched hand and ran on. Abigail turned to go down. Cindy and Ramona were still beside her. The other rabbits were hopping around the rocks.

'Stay here with the others and don't move,' said Abigail, raising her wand.

Ramona looked at Cindy. 'Quick, dig out those small stones and flick them over to me,' she said, suddenly getting an idea. 'We'll kick them at the crones.' Ramona turned to the other rabbits. 'Bunnies, get ready to fire!' The other rabbits lined up, turned sideways and waited for Cindy.

The cat rummaged around and gathered some small stones. Then, leaning on her front paws, she scratched and dug with her back paws, flicking the pile of stones off the ground in the rabbits' direction. The skilful rabbits kicked the flying stones straight at the crones with their strong back legs. They soon got into a rhythm and the crones yelped in pain as they were peppered with pebbles and stones.

The rabbits' little plan was soon spotted and they all had to dive for cover when they were hit by a barrage of spells.

Further down the rocks, Luke, Jamie and the other pets were in trouble.

'Jamie, I'm out of arrows,' cried Luke, 'and most of the pets are injured. Look!'

Trigger was lying on his side. Dougal was whimpering. His ears and nose had been burned by a spell. Cyril's wing was broken when he was walloped by a broom. The sparrows' stunning beaks were freezing the crones' arms and hands so that they couldn't use their wands, but the little birds were worn out. Oberon was pulling the crones off their brooms by tugging at their capes from behind. Some of them landed on the rocks, some got trapped in the poisonous seaweed, others fell to the demons of the deep.

'We have to use a gemstone,' said Luke. 'We're destroying lots of them, but there are so many, we can't get them all.'

'Do it,' said Jamie. 'Use the next one. Hold it tight

and think of turning them to dust.'

Luke broke off the next stone, the amethyst. He closed his fist around it and wished, but he forgot to close his eyes. He heard Trigger whimpering in pain. He looked at him for a second and when he opened his hand the gemstone was gone, but nothing happened to the crones.

'Ha ha,' screamed a crone. 'The charms don't work unless you're very certain. You've missed your chance. Ahh ha ha ha!'

She swung away on her broomstick to spread the word. The crones cackled loudly, delighted that Luke had made such an awful mistake.

'Oh, no, no, NO!' cried Luke. 'I'm sorry! I was looking at Trigger. NO!'

'Luke, forget it. Go back to Grindlewood and get Ernie,' shouted Jamie.

'What?' said Luke.

'We can use a gemstone to give Ernie his healing powers again,' said Jamie. 'Wanda chose him to be a healer before – it's our best chance!'

Luke hesitated. He was still flustered at having made a mess of his wish.

'You have the brooch in your pocket. GO!' cried Jamie.

Luke scrambled over the sand dunes and ran to where he had drawn the circle. He jumped inside and pushed the diamond back in. He was back in Grindlewood, and it was still afternoon. 'That was lucky,' he thought, 'but what time will it be when I go back to the west?'

He ran to the pond. Sylvie and the Brigadier trotted over to him. They could tell something was wrong. Luke was sure the animals could understand him, so he explained what had happened as he tried to find Ernie.

The frog was asleep and hidden from sight. The Brigadier saw that Luke was frantic and so he jumped into the water. He made as much noise as possible to wake their froggy friend.

'Hello,' said Ernie, when he finally popped up. 'What are you doing in here?'

'Ernie, Luke needs your help, they all do,' said the Brigadier, spluttering and splashing. 'They're in trouble in the west. They need to restore your powers so you can heal everyone. Some of the residents are badly hurt.'

'You don't mind going back with him, do you Ernie?' asked Sylvie from the edge of the pond.

'Of course not!' said the big warty frog. 'Let's go!' He hopped across the lily pads and out of the pond.

Luke took out the next gemstone, an opal. He closed his fist around it and thought only of Ernie and his magical healing powers. When he opened his eyes, the gemstone was gone and Ernie was still looking at him.

'Well?' said Luke hopefully. Ernie just said, 'Ribbit'. Luke said a quick goodbye to the Brigadier and Sylvie, grabbed the frog, ran to the circle, jumped in and pulled out the western diamond. In a flash, they were gone.

Chapter Seventeen

THE BOOK OF WISDOM

Timber ran quickly through the labyrinth of caves. He was surprised to suddenly pick up Gildevard's scent, and he knew it could only mean trouble.

The eagle had been stupified by the crones and then shoved into a small cage. He could expect to become part of their supper. When Timber reached the edge of the innermost cave, he stopped to look at the book. The crones had left it where Gildevard had dropped it on the ground.

'Timber, help, get me out of here,' croaked the eagle from the back of the cave.

'What are you doing here, Gildevard?' barked Timber, looking up.

'I'll tell you everything. Just get me out of here!' cried the eagle.

'I'm here to take this book back to the Forest Queen,' said Timber, placing his paw on it. 'She asked for our help.'

'Did she? Who's with you?' asked Gildevard.

'Most of the residents and the children too,' said the big dog. 'There's a terrible fight going on outside. I have to take this book out of here and help the others.'

'You'll need the children to do that,' said the eagle. 'I tried to lift it but it was too heavy. And Kelvin betrayed me, the little wretch. We're all in a lot of trouble now.'

Timber tried lifting the book in his mouth, but it was too awkward to hold for more than a few seconds. He went over to the cage, sniffed at it and growled. He gripped the lock and shook it hard, but it didn't budge.

'You'll have to get the key,' said Gildevard. 'The old crone with three eyes has it. Her legs are bad, so she's probably near the fire on the beach.'

'First the book, then I might come back for you,' said Timber crossly. He turned and ran all the way out – straight into Jemima. She had finally reached the top of the rocks. He jumped on her, again and again, barking for her to follow him. She gingerly entered the caves, checking the map, hoping they wouldn't somehow get lost or ambushed along the way. They went all the way in without any trouble.

'*The Book of Wisdom*,' cried Jemima, 'and the golden eagle. What's he doing here?'

Gildevard gave a weak squawk and Timber pawed the book on the floor. Jemima picked it up. She staggered sideways and it slipped out of her hands. It was much heavier than she had expected. 'I won't be able to carry this and that cage. What'll I do?' she thought.

Timber barked at Jemima, and kept barking until she got the message. She had to take the book. She bent down and picked it up. She gripped it as tightly as she could and slowly walked out. If she could just get it out of the caves, then one of the others could help her, while another could return for the eagle. Timber trotted out beside her as the eagle watched them go.

Outside, the mayhem continued. Luke had returned with Ernie and it was time to test the magic. Thankfully, the gemstone had worked. The frog healed Trigger and Dougal first and then Dougal ran around the other injured birds and animals with the frog clinging to his collar. Trigger stayed near Luke, returning to his job of collecting any arrows that could be reused.

Jamie's skill with the sword was improving every minute. The ring flashed as he fought several crones at once, spinning around to catch them above and beside him, knocking them out, cutting wands, chopping brooms, slashing capes, turning many to dust. But somehow the crones kept coming.

Abigail had finally found the courage to use her wand.

'Stupificus totalis!' she cried, and a crone froze in mid-leap and then collapsed. Abigail kept repeating the spell on every crone close by, making it easier for Luke and Jamie to knock them out completely.

Timber and Jemima emerged from the caves. It was awkward, scrambling down the rocks with the book. Jemima had to go very slowly. Timber ran ahead of her, barking more instructions.

'Trigger, make Luke go up to the top of these rocks. He must take the book from Jemima. It's too heavy for her. She might fall.' Trigger jumped all over Luke, until he understood, then dashed ahead of him, scrambling over the rocks towards Jemima.

'Protectum tinitum!' cried Abigail, using spell number two. Although she hadn't quite perfected it yet, she was hoping it might protect Dougal and Ernie as they ran around the wounded. For a few seconds, a protective veil covered the dog and frog as they raced around. Then it popped, and Abigail repeated it again and again, in between casting her other spell.

'Stupificus totalis!' she cried as another squadron of crones on brooms appeared. And then there were more and still more. Hundreds must have been asleep in other caves, and now they were all coming to attack.

A few crones crept quietly up behind Abigail. She was concentrating so hard on her spells that she didn't hear them. As they prepared to cast a blitzing spell to put a final stop to her magic, Abigail heard Teddy's loud meow nearby. She turned and gasped in fright, but it was the crones who screamed loudest.

'Aaahhh, Wanda's wand! Aaahhhh!'

When they recognised the wand, they couldn't

get away fast enough, knocking and pushing each other down the rocks. Some were smashed on jagged boulders and turned to dust. One or two bounced further down and were devoured by a huge black serpent that slithered out of the waves. It retreated with its supper.

'Well done, Teddy,' barked Timber. 'Now follow me. We have to get a key!'

'What key?' called Teddy as he raced after him.

'Gildevard is trapped in a cage and one of the crones has the key.'

'What?' cried Eldric, as Timber and Teddy raced by. The fox and rabbits had been following Abigail as she continued down the rocks. Jemima and Luke were higher up but they were making their way down too. Luke carried the book and Trigger was running alongside them. Jamie was chasing a group of crones over boulders and rocks, picking them off one by one.

The Grindlewood Army gathered quickly near the huge cauldron. The birds stayed close together. The animals prowled around, growling and hissing at a few old hags around the fire. Most of the remaining crones had run off when they got wind of Wanda's wand. They watched from a distance.

'Get back, get back!' cried the three-eyed crone, stabbing her wand in the air.

Abigail raised her wand, preparing to cast her freezing spell.

'That beginners' spell won't work on me. I'm immune to it, and the others will come out of it soon. What'll you do then?' said the crone, spitting from her jagged teeth. 'You're outnumbered and outclassed. Bah!'

'We'll be long gone,' said Jamie, and he sliced the crone's wand in two.

'Aaahhhh, my wand! It was two hundred years old. How dare you!'

She was so busy screeching, she didn't notice Teddy had crawled under her cloak. He quickly found the keys. Timber followed him, much to the crone's surprise, as she fell over with the force of his charge. He picked up the keys in his mouth and dropped them at Jamie's feet.

'We have the book!' shrieked Jemima, stumbling onto the beach at last. Luke was a few steps behind her, holding it tightly.

'We have it!' he cried.

'Yeeess!' said Jamie.

'Great!' said Abigail. 'Let's get out of here.'

Timber was barking loudly at Jamie. He jumped on him, pawed the keys, then jumped on him again.

'What are those?' said Jamie, picking up the bunch of keys. Timber kept barking.

'Jamie, the eagle is up there in the cave where I found the book,' said Jemima. 'He's stuck in a cage.'

'Then one of these keys must open it,' said Jamie. Timber barked again and ran towards the rocks. He stopped and looked back, hoping Jamie would follow. 'I'll go and get him,' said Jamie. 'Timber, show me where he is.'

Jamie followed Timber over the rocks as quickly as he could. The others remained below, watching to see if any more crones came out of the freezing spell. Some of them were looking a little less stupefied, just like the three-eyed crone had said. Others were starting to come gingerly out of hiding.

'Jamie, meet us at the circle,' called Luke.

'OK, you go on,' Jamie shouted back.

As Jamie and Timber headed for the cave, the others ran across the beach, tripping over bones, bottles and pots, around the rocks and bushes, over the sand dunes, back to where they had arrived.

When they reached the circle, they huddled together inside the magical line. The Grindlewood butterflies had been sleeping nearby the whole time. They were perched on a thorny bush just outside the circle.

'I wonder why they came with us this time,' said Jemima. 'They're just sitting there.'

'Maybe they were told to watch,' said Luke.

'I wish Jamie would hurry,' said Abigail. 'We really need to get out of here.'

Then there was more trouble. The stupified crones fell out of the freezing spell all at once, and Jamie, Timber and Gildevard were only just emerging from the cave.

'What'll we do? My spells aren't strong enough to hold them off,' cried Abigail.

'Do them again, and keep doing them,' cried Luke.

'Stupificus totalis! Stupificus totalis! Oh, this is hopeless! Why isn't it working?'

'Try another one, any one,' said Luke, loading an arrow.

'Look! I can see them. They're coming!' cried Jemima. 'They've got the eagle. Jamie, hurry, hurry!'

'Come on, Jamie, come on!' cried Luke. He fired more arrows.

Trigger, Dougal and Eldric barked to Timber to hurry. Teddy and Cindy were meowing. The crones were gathering again, cackling and laughing, their wands at the ready.

'They're going to catch them, Luke, what'll we do?' cried Jemima.

'Jamie, hurry, we have to leave NOW!' cried Luke. He was looking at his watch. It was two minutes to seven.

Carrying the injured eagle in the cage in one hand and his sword in the other meant the climb down the rocks was slow and awkward. And Jamie knew they had very little time left.

'Go, Luke!' cried Jamie. 'Get them home and come back for us! GO!'

In that instant, Luke knew Jamie was right. They had only one minute left. Suddenly, he had another idea. He had to be quick. He broke off another gemstone from the string. He clasped his fist around the aquamarine, closed his eyes and wished. The stone vanished. He opened his eyes and stared at the butterflies. But nothing happened.

Luke took the brooch out of his pocket. His hands shook and the girls gasped as he pushed in the western diamond – and they were gone.

The children and pets arrived in Grindlewood garden in a terrible state.

'What about Jamie, Timber and Gildevard?' cried Jemima.

'Luke, what did you wish for?' asked Abigail.

'I wished for the butterflies to use whatever magic they have to save Jamie, Timber and Gildevard, once we were gone,' said Luke, 'but I'm not sure if that's in the rules.'

'We have to go back right away,' cried Jemima.

'We can't,' said Luke. 'It's too late.'

Chapter Eighteen

THE GREAT ESCAPE

Jamie, Timber and Gildevard were in a lot of trouble. They hid amongst the rocks, hoping to dodge a wave of spells that cracked and sizzled as they bounced off the rocks and scorched clumps of dry grass. The crones fired on them from all angles – some from the beach, some from the rocks, others as they whizzed overhead on their brooms. A few had moved to the cauldron. They were chanting spells and arguing over who would get to toss the three visitors into the pot.

Jamie didn't know what to do. They weren't going to last long if they stayed where they were, and if they tried to run, they would be easy targets. His sword was still in his hand. It was all he had to save them. He looked at Timber and pulled him close. He loved him so much and he didn't want him to die.

After a moment, Timber stood up and started growling again. Slowly Jamie turned his head to see what had caught the dog's attention. He knew it couldn't be anything good. He was right. Some of the stronger crones had climbed up the rocks and found them. Jamie couldn't see any of them yet, but he could smell them and then he could hear them.

Jamie took a deep breath and jumped out, his sword shining brightly as it caught the light of the huge full moon. Timber barked and ran around him. He attacked the crones bravely, jumping into the first three as they appeared over a boulder. Jamie stood beside his dog and swung his sword. Two more crones clambered into view and were swiftly knocked back. But again, there were just too many. They were coming in droves.

As the crones closed in, Jamie and Timber were repeatedly burned and cut by spells. Timber was determined to protect his master, leaping and jumping bravely all around him. Jamie twisted and turned, fighting as hard as he could. But then disaster struck – his foot caught in a small gap between the rocks. He groaned and fell. It was a bad sprain. Timber jumped in front of him, his barks sounding more and more hoarse, he was so determined to protect his master. Jamie wriggled around on the ground, trying to free his foot. It ached so badly, but he still struck out from the ground at every crone within reach.

Suddenly the crones stopped attacking. They shrieked and cowered, and slowly backed away. They were looking past Jamie and Timber at something, something that scared them. Timber turned quickly to see what it was. Jamie took the chance to try to free his foot, roaring in pain as he pulled it out of the gap. He managed to stand up, leaning on his sword, and then he looked around.

An incredible transformation had taken place out of sight, but now it was clear for everyone to see. The three enchanted butterflies had grown gigantic. Jamie stared at all the details, now so clear: the large, dark round eyes, slim mouth, wide nostrils and huge antennae bobbing about on their foreheads. The rainbow wings were dazzling, like giant coloured cloaks billowing in the wind. The flapping sounded more like a roar as they rose in the air, striking terror into the crones. Those on broomsticks flew quickly to the safety of the caves. Those on the rocks tried to hide.

Timber sniffed the air and wagged his tail. He too knew what they were.

'Look at our butterflies,' whispered Jamie, as they landed close by and folded their wings. They waited.

'Really?' said Jamie. 'You want us to get up there? OK, eh, how do we hold on?' Timber jumped on Jamie, prodded the eagle's cage with his nose and barked. They didn't really have time to think about it. Suddenly, Jamie understood. He took the eagle out of his cage and placed him gently on the back of one butterfly. Hopefully he would be able to cling on with his talons. The butterfly nodded, his antennae swinging gently to and fro. The eagle sank into the softness of the butterfly's back.

'OK, that works,' said Jamie. 'Timber, you're next.' He helped his dog scramble up onto another butterfly, spreading his paws to balance his weight. The second butterfly nodded. Timber sank into the butterfly, like he was sitting on a huge pillow.

'My turn,' said Jamie, as he climbed onto the third one and leaned forward, wrapping his arms around the butterfly's neck. It was surprisingly comfortable. Then the three giant insects opened their wings and took to the air.

'Wow!' cried Jamie, again and again. After a few nervous minutes, the three passengers relaxed into the soft bodies of the magical butterflies. It was a beautiful night flight back to Grindlewood.

A few hours later, they landed safely in the middle of the garden. It was late and dark and a heavy drizzle was falling. The children ran out of the fairy house. Luke and Jemima had told their parents something about a late picnic in the garden. Abigail had phoned home but there was no answer. And so they waited in the garden, hoping.

The children were speechless as they watched Jamie slide down the side of a giant butterfly. His ankle was sore and swollen and he winced as he jumped onto the grass. He helped Timber down and then took Gildevard and hobbled over to Ernie. The frog started healing Timber's wounds first and then hopped over to the eagle, who was quickly restored.

'That was some escape!' said Luke, as they watched the butterflies shrink back to normal. They fluttered down the garden into the darkness as if nothing had happened.

'It was incredible,' said Jamie.

'Jamie, your ankle!' cried Jemima. 'Will Ernie be able to fix it?'

'I'm not sure. I didn't like how it felt the last time he healed me, but it's worth a try. Ouch!' Jamie sat on the grass and Ernie hopped all over his ankle and foot. After a few 'ows' and 'ouches' the swelling went down and his ankle felt a lot better.

'What was it like flying?' asked Jemima.

'Absolutely amazing,' said Jamie. 'At first I was terrified we would fall off, but it was like lying on a big beanbag!'

'It'll take a lot of memory mist to cover this up!' said Luke.

'It's probably falling in the drizzle,' said Abigail. 'That should take care of it.'

'Em, what happened with all those crones?' asked Jemima.

'They attacked us again, loads of them,' said Jamie. 'The butterflies came to the rescue just in time.'

'Jamie, I'm really sorry we left like that,' said Luke. 'When we arrived back here, it was too late to go back for you. I was hoping the gemstone would get you out of there after we left.'

'Well it did,' said Jamie. 'It was very clever. I knew

it was too late for you to come back, but I never expected such a crazy escape.'

'We were really worried about you,' said Jemima, giving Jamie a hug.

'Thanks,' said Jamie. 'I was worried for a while too. Hey, where's the book?'

'It's in the fairy house,' said Abigail.

'Let's bring it to the queen in the morning,' said Luke. 'I don't think any of us want to see her right now.'

'She'll probably be asleep now, anyway,' said Jemima, yawning.

'Let's bring it into the main house,' said Jamie. 'I'd like to know that it's beside us during the night.'

The others agreed. They went into the fairy house to talk for a few minutes. Outside, Timber told the waiting residents the whole story. Then he turned to Gildevard.

'Why didn't you tell us what you were up to?' barked Timber.

'This was a personal matter,' said the eagle. 'It had nothing to do with Grindlewood. Anyway, I didn't know about the quest.'

Timber glared at him. 'Of course it has something

to do with Grindlewood,' he said. 'The WABOM belongs to the Wandeleis and they have lived here for centuries. Wanda left those treasures here, so we could use them to find the WABOM and return it to its rightful owner. But I think *you* were planning to *steal* it.'

'Now just a minute,' said Gildevard.

'We know there was something else written on the scroll,' interrupted Oberon, 'and we also know that you made a deal with Bodric.'

The golden eagle scowled.

'I admit that I was tempted by all the knowledge in that book, but I didn't mean any harm,' he said. 'I only wanted to take a look.'

'Do you really expect us to believe that?' barked Timber. 'You lied to us about the scroll.'

'Timber, everyone, I am sorry about that,' said Gildevard, but he was struggling to *sound* sorry.

'I hope so,' said Timber. 'We'll talk again in the morning.'

Timber snorted a few times and scraped his paws on the ground. It was time for the night patrol. He and Teddy would do it quickly and then go inside to guard the book. The residents all went their own way, chattering about what had happened and relieved that everyone was safe. Several of them snarled at Gildevard as they passed by.

'You may sleep in the loft if you wish,' said Oberon, 'but don't talk to me, Gildevard. I am far too annoyed with you to have a conversation.' And the owl flew off to hunt.

After talking over the day's events, the children went into the house. Some sandwiches and biscuits were still on the table. They hadn't noticed how hungry they were until they saw the food. Luke and Abigail were going to sleep over as they would be heading to Hollow Hill early the next morning. Luke rang his parents again to say he was staying with the Grindles. They were obviously still under the *Agreeable* spell, as Jamie called it, because they didn't mind at all.

Abigail was getting worried, though. She couldn't understand why there was no answer at home. She knew now that sometimes her mum and granddad had to go out at night on magic business, but usually one of them was there. Something was niggling her, but it would have to wait till tomorrow.

Jamie took *The Book of Wisdom* into his room. They

were all too tired to care what was in it. They simply had to go to sleep. The girls went into Jemima's room, and straight to bed. Teddy snuggled up on the bean bag in the corner, exhausted. Cindy purred and curled up on the duvet.

Timber, Trigger and Dougal followed the boys into Jamie's room. The boys were asleep in minutes, but the dogs took turns to guard the book all through the night.

Chapter Nineteen

TENSE TIMES

Everyone slept soundly that night. The children woke to the delicious smell of pancakes wafting up from the kitchen. The pets were already awake, sitting around *The Book of Wisdom*, Timber with his nose and paws on top of it.

They all went downstairs together. Jamie carried the book.

'Oh, that looks very grand,' said Gloria as they entered the kitchen. 'Is that another one of Mr Allnutt's books?'

'Eh, no, sort of, eh,' muttered Jamie.

'It's one that Granddad told us about, Mrs Grindle,' said Abigail.

'We're just going to take a look at it now, Mum,' said Jemima.

'And we might take the dogs for a walk,' said Luke.

'Have fun, then,' said Gloria.

'I still can't get used to that,' said Jamie. 'If only it was always so easy to get away with stuff.'

'It's a great bit of magic, isn't it?' said Luke, grinning.

'You should definitely learn it as soon as possible, Abby,' said Jamie.

'Good plan!' said Luke. 'Come on, it's time to visit the queen.'

Timber and the children went through the trap door in the fairy house, down the ladder and along the tunnel. When they arrived in Hollow Hill, they were hoping the queen would be more cheerful than the last time. They weren't disappointed.

'Oh, you have done well!' said the queen.

It was the first time she had smiled warmly. Timber trotted over and sat at the base of the trunk as the queen opened the book. She was delighted to see the beautiful old parchment, its wise and solemn words and intricate artwork. The professors were very excited too.

'This is wonderful, simply wonderful!' said Sparks.

'That's three out of four,' said Flint. 'I can hardly believe it!'

'Well done, children, Timber,' said Pendrick. 'We cannot thank you enough. Now that we have *The Book of Wisdom*, we should be able to complete the spell that reverses the curse.'

'At last,' said the queen. 'Thank you, children.'

Jamie looked at her. He was beginning to understand what only Timber had seen before. Deep down the queen was kind and gentle, or at least she had been. But her softness didn't last long.

'So, why didn't you return the book last night? We have lost another day!' she said.

'The children didn't all arrive back together, Your Majesty. Timber, Jamie and the eagle came back later, by butterfly,' said Pendrick.

'By butterfly?' said the queen. 'So you needed more magic. How many gemstones have you used?'

'Four,' said Jamie. Luke held up his wrist to show her.

'What? Four?' roared the queen. 'Don't you realise that you have only three left, but you have half of the WABOM still to return? You have been foolish!'

'But we already know where *The Book of Light* is,'

~ 239 ~

said Luke sheepishly, 'and then there is only *The Book of Darkness* left …'

'Only *The Book of Darkness*!' cried the queen. 'All of the books are equally precious, but your final task will be the most difficult. And we have traitors in our midst. Do not waste the magic!' The queen looked like she might burst into flames. Her face was bright red and her hair was standing on end. A final shower of dead leaves fell from her shaking branches, leaving her bare.

'I will explain it again,' said Pendrick. 'Be careful with the String of Charms, children. As time passes, our magic will continue to weaken until it is no more. Those gemstones really are all we have left to help you.'

'It was my fault,' said Luke. 'I wasted one because my thoughts weren't clear. I was worried about my dog.'

Timber woo-wooed softly at the queen. She stroked his ears and calmed down.

'Never mind,' she said. 'What's done is done. You must prepare for the journey north. Don't expect the buzzard to give up *The Book of Darkness* too easily. Remember to use the gemstones carefully and keep one in reserve, just in case.'

They left with the professors and walked silently back to the reception chamber. The only sound was Timber's paws pad-padding on the ground. Everyone was thinking about Bodric Buzzard and what lay ahead in the north.

'Children and Timber,' said Pendrick, 'I don't want to alarm you, but the Renewal Charm can only be performed at dawn on Halloween morning. That is two days from tomorrow. Please, try your hardest to find the final part of the WABOM and return it quickly. You won't get a second chance. None of us will.'

'We'll do our very best, Professor,' said Luke.

'What's so special about Halloween?' asked Jamie.

'It is tradition that the new queen must be named on Halloween morning and begin her reign immediately,' said Flint.

'Who is the next queen?' asked Jemima.

'We don't know,' said Sparks, 'but we hope the queen has someone in mind.'

'Will you really be able to break the tree curse?' asked Abigail.

'We hope so, my dear,' said Pendrick. 'Your mother

and grandfather were helping us last night. I told them you were going to be late.'

The children looked puzzled.

'All the butterflies are connected,' explained Pendrick. 'When one trio performs magic, the other butterflies know this and tell us. When we heard there was magic at work in the west, we knew that you would all arrive back safely – even if three of you were a little late.'

'Wow!' said Jamie. 'That's amazing!'

'Even as a wizard, magic still surprises me sometimes,' said Pendrick with a smile. 'Now, go home and relax. You can't go north without instruction, so come back here at three o'clock this afternoon and we'll have a chat about your final task.'

Pendrick twirled around and headed off down one of the side tunnels. The children and Timber went home and straight to their collection of books.

'We need to find out more about Bodric Buzzard and his army,' said Jemima.

'And *The Book of Darkness*,' said Jamie.

'I don't like the sound of it,' said Luke. 'I hope it's not booby-trapped.'

'I found something about it the other day. We were

so busy I forgot to tell you,' said Abigail. 'Here, look, in *The History of Magic, Volume VII*:

> *To be truly good and wise, we must understand evil, and in particular, how to control it. We learn that from The Book of Darkness.*

'That sounds OK,' said Jamie.

'There's more,' said Abigail.

'Of course there is,' said Luke. 'It couldn't be that simple.'

Abigail continued:

> *The Book of Darkness teaches the dark arts. It is intended only for those already well versed in magic: highly trained, skilful and honourable students. It is not for the faint-hearted, the weak-minded or those who seek magic for personal gain or power. In such hands it would be a dangerous tool. The Book of Darkness also instructs on punishments, banishing spells, alternate dimensions, Warlock Hell, the Vortex and the Outer Oblivion. These lessons are strictly for the most exceptionally skilled magicians of mature and sound character. Higher examinations must be passed with a gold star of achievement before*

progressing to these final chapters.

'That's heavy,' said Luke.

'It sounds really serious,' said Jemima.

'Granddad said it is,' said Abigail. 'We have to be careful with *The Book of Darkness*, really careful.'

'Then the sooner we take it away from that evil buzzard, the better,' said Jamie.

'Granddad also said we should take the crystal key with us this time,' said Abigail.

'Then we will,' said Jemima.

'But we've managed without it so far,' said Luke.

'Only just about,' said Abigail. 'Jamie and Timber and the eagle could have been killed.'

'Or trapped in another dimension with the crones, for ever!' said Jemima.

'Maybe we should take it, Luke,' said Jamie. 'I don't want to annoy the queen, especially with that collar on Timber, but the journey north is going to be the most difficult yet and we have to get *The Book of Darkness* to finish this.'

They all looked at Luke. He was trying to be sensible but perhaps he was too cautious.

'Let's think about it and decide just before we go, OK?' said Luke.

The others agreed.

❦

Timber wanted to know more about Bodric too. He called a meeting and the residents gathered at the end of the garden, beside the granite stone. They were still very cross with the eagle and it was hard to move off the subject.

'Jamie and Timber could have been killed trying to rescue you!' snarled Eldric.

'I told you I didn't know you were looking for the WABOM,' said Gildevard. 'I only wanted to see *The Book of Wisdom*. I knew I could never keep it. I just wanted to take a look.'

'Nonsense!' said the Brigadier. 'Anyway, who would have rescued you if we hadn't … I mean if Timber hadn't?'

'Thank you, Timber. I am extremely grateful to you and Jamie.' Gildevard was trying to remain polite but he was growing tired of these comments. He tried to change the subject. 'I was betrayed by my apprentice, you know.'

'That was another mistake you made,' said Eldric. 'Imagine trusting a kestrel.'

The eagle sighed.

'What is Kelvin up to?' asked Timber.

'I don't know,' said the eagle. 'He came with me to the Crabbage Caves, *pretending* to help me, but he must be working for Bodric instead.'

'What would he want with the book?' asked Timber.

'I really don't know,' said Gildevard.

'I heard him mention Zora, a sorceress,' said Oberon. 'Do you know who that is?'

'Oh,' said the eagle, 'if magical people are involved, we must be very careful.'

'We?' said Timber.

'I thought perhaps I could help,' said the eagle, 'if you'll let me.'

'Why not?' said Timber. 'That way we'll know exactly what you're up to. Now, who is Zora?'

Chapter Twenty

INTRUDERS!

The rest of the day seemed long, and all anyone could think about was the end of the quest. As there were few people they could talk to about it, and they had a couple of hours to spare, the children decided to visit the Allnutts. The animals and birds were down at the end of the garden and the children knew that another meeting must be taking place.

'Let's leave them here,' said Jemima. 'They need some time off too.'

'Good idea,' said Jamie. 'Timber probably has a lot to tell them.'

The children were feeling more relaxed as they strolled down the road to the village. They chatted and laughed about lots of things, things they hadn't had time to think or talk about for a while. But when they arrived at Abigail's house, they got a dreadful shock.

The hall door was open, yet no one seemed to be in. Abigail called three times to her mum and her granddad but there was no reply. She was about to go in but Jamie stopped her at the doorway.

'Wait,' he said, 'just in case.' Jamie took out his sword and swished it back and forth to prepare the magic. Gorlan's ring flashed on his finger. He walked slowly inside, looking left, right and straight ahead, watching for someone, anyone. Luke was right behind him, carefully looking and listening too. The girls followed. Abigail pulled out her wand from under her coat.

It was clear that the house had been vandalised. Books and papers were strewn everywhere, pictures had been pulled off the walls and destroyed and furniture was knocked over. The kitchen was in an even bigger mess. Windows had been broken and all the crockery had been taken out of the cupboards and smashed. They stopped moving for a moment and listened. They could just make out the muffled sound of voices coming from the cellar.

They tiptoed down and peeped around the door.

Abigail's granddad was lying in a heap. Esther was kneeling beside him and Professor Pendrick was mumbling healing spells, trying to use any last bit of magic he had to save Thaddeus.

'Oh, no, Mr Allnutt!' cried Jamie. Abigail pushed past to see what was wrong.

'Granddad! Mum, what happened?' she cried.

'Abigail, children, we were attacked last night when we returned from Hollow Hill. Someone was waiting here for us. I was knocked out by a blitzing spell. When I woke up in the hall a little while ago, I found the house topsy turvy and your granddad lying here. I sent our nightingale with a message to Pendrick.'

Esther had a nasty cut on her temple where the blitzing spell had struck her, but she was more concerned about Thaddeus.

'Pendrick, can you help him?'

'I'm trying, Esther, but my magic is so weak that I can't do very much at all. We need something stronger, and quickly.'

'They must have been looking for *The Book of Light*,' said Jamie.

'Probably,' said Esther. 'Oh, the chest! Where is it? It's been moved.' Esther and the boys looked around.

Esther bit her lip and put her arm around Abigail.

'The stones!' cried Jemima, suddenly. 'Use one of the gemstones!'

'Yes!' cried Jamie.

'Can we? Please?' said Abigail.

'Will it work?' asked Esther, looking at the professor.

'Perhaps,' he replied, 'but it means you will have one less gemstone for tomorrow.'

'We have to save Granddad,' cried Abigail.

'Of course, dear,' said Esther gently, 'but we can't be sure it will work.'

'It is our best chance,' said Pendrick.

'Let's do it,' said Jamie.

'The next one is the sapphire,' said Luke, unclipping it. He held it out.

'One of you must do it,' said Pendrick. 'The stones are for you, remember?'

'I'll do it, Abby,' said Jamie. 'You might be a little, em, upset.'

Esther and Pendrick nodded.

Jamie took the stone and held it tightly. He closed his eyes and thought only of healing Abigail's granddad. When he opened his eyes the sapphire was gone. They watched and waited. Slowly, slowly, Thaddeus came around. Blinking and coughing, he tried to sit up. A rosy glow returned to his cheeks.

'It worked!' cried Jemima.

'Take it slowly, now,' said Pendrick, as he lifted his friend into a sitting position. 'You're in the cellar, Thaddeus.'

'What? Where are those devils? Where are they?'

'Who was it, Thaddeus?' asked Esther. 'Who did this?'

'Traitors,' said Thaddeus. 'They didn't find it, did they?'

'No,' said Pendrick. 'The book is still here.'

'Oh, thank heavens!'

'Do you remember anything at all?' asked Esther. 'I was knocked out when I opened the front door. All I saw was a cloaked figure in the dark.'

'I was in the cellar, looking through a few of my books when I heard the doorbell. You answered the door, Esther. I heard the blitzing spell. I grabbed my wand, intending to run up the stairs, but …' Thaddeus stopped.

'And then?' said Jamie.

'I remember duelling with a cloaked figure,' said Thaddeus, 'but there was someone or something else charging around upstairs, searching for the book, I suppose.'

'Once we were both knocked out, the two of them must have continued ransacking the place,' said Esther.

Thaddeus tried to smile at the concerned faces around him. Pendrick and Esther helped him up and they moved slowly up to the kitchen. After a mug of sweet tea, Thaddeus looked a lot better, but something was bothering him, something important.

'Don't worry, it'll come back to you,' said Pendrick. 'Thank goodness we had some real magic to save you.'

'You didn't use a gemstone on me, did you?' said Thaddeus. 'You'll need them up north against Bodric and his army. You'll need every bit of magic we have.'

'Of course we did, Granddad,' said Abigail, giving him a hug.

'They still have two left, Thaddeus, and you really needed one,' said Esther.

'I had better get back to Hollow Hill,' said Pendrick. 'The queen needs to hear about this, and Flint and Sparks too.'

'Don't tell anyone else, will you?' said Thaddeus quickly. 'We can't be certain who we can trust, not after this.'

'I know,' said Pendrick. 'I'll check on you later, Thaddeus. Goodbye for now.' Pendrick hurried down to the cellar and disappeared through the trap door.

⁕

'I know he has it! I just know it!' cried a rasping voice under a grey hood.

'But we didn't find it!' replied the small animal sitting in the corner. 'How could he hide it with so little magic left?'

'Because, my little friend, he hid it when his magic was powerful!'

The third creature in the room growled at the little furry animal. Dwarf-trolls were always bad tempered.

'Bodric won't be pleased,' said Ripley. 'What are you going to do, Audmund?'

'I will get *The Book of Light* once I have fully restored the magic in Worfeus' wand,' said Audmund. 'It's a powerful wand and I can tell that it likes me.'

'Well, it's a plan, I suppose,' said Ripley, 'but don't forget my reward for finding the wand. How careless of those children to just toss it into the field behind their garden.' The squirrel sniggered until Audmund couldn't bear it any longer.

'Quiet, Ripley,' said Audmund. 'Worfeus found *The Book of Potions and Spells* with this exceptional wand, did he not?' said the augurer, admiring the wand in his hand.

'I believe so,' said Ripley.

'Then that is how I will find *The Book of Light* – the *precise* location. Then my big, ugly friend here will get it for me. But remember, Ripley, time is short. If the children and those animals complete the quest, Zora will not be pleased.'

'Do you think she plans to destroy Grindlewood?' asked Ripley.

'I expect so,' said Audmund, with an evil smirk on his face. 'I hope so.'

'And what of Bodric, Audmund, what will happen to him after, you know?' asked Ripley. The dwarf-troll in the corner roared and beat his chest with his fists like an angry gorilla.

'QUIET, Grizzle!' cried Audmund. The growling stopped. 'I'll deal with Bodric, Ripley. Leave him to me.'

'And Vargon?'

'He won't last much longer either.'

Chapter Twenty-one

PREPARING FOR NORTH

The residents gathered to talk about their next task. Oberon explained everything he knew about Bodric's army of vicious hawks and scavenging buzzards. On his brief visit north a few days before, he had spotted a few Worfagon warlocks there too. After the defeat of Worfeus, they had ended up in Bodric's camp. No one really knew much more about them. Timber wanted to know more about the sorceress and he pressed Gildevard for an answer.

'Well? Have you heard of her?' he asked.

'I do remember hearing something, though I can't be sure it was about the same person, you understand,' said the eagle.

'Go on,' said Timber.

'There was a rumour that Worfeus wasn't meant to

rule alone after his father died,' said the eagle.

'We never heard that before,' said Teddy, looking at Timber.

'Some say that the young warlock was meant to share power with his sister, a twin, but she vanished right after their father's funeral. Worfeus claimed that she had died of a broken heart; others weren't convinced. Either way, she never returned, so Worfeus ruled alone.'

'Do you think the story is true?' asked Timber.

'It's possible, but it was before my time,' said Gildevard.

'I'd say Worfeus got rid of her,' said Norville. 'He was a nasty piece of work.'

'There was something else about a pet bird,' said the eagle. 'Apparently, she found it injured and decided to keep it.'

'A bird!' said Oberon. 'Could it have been Bodric?'

'The story gets a bit fuzzy, but I heard that she enchanted her pet bird with the ability to talk to her through thoughts.'

'An ideal spy,' said Timber.

'I suppose so,' said Gildevard. 'The charm is called

Mind-melding and it uses very dark magic.'

'Would that magic still be as powerful after all this time?' asked Oberon.

'I don't know,' said the eagle.

'Why would Zora want to come back here?' asked Dougal.

'Who knows?' said the eagle. 'But it might explain the frantic race for the WABOM.'

'What would she want with the WABOM?' asked Teddy.

'Power?' suggested Timber.

'Or revenge,' said Gildevard.

Oberon nodded. 'The Wandeleis' magic is the oldest and purest magic ever known. Many seek its true source, believing it will make them all-knowledgeable and all-powerful. The WABOM might reveal the source of that power or hold clues to finding it.'

'I have a bad feeling about this,' muttered Norville.

'More secrets and mysteries,' muttered Eldric.

'We travel north tomorrow,' said Timber, 'and we won't find answers to all those questions before then. Never mind. Let's go over our plan again, and when we're finished, I want to hear what the children are planning too.'

Early the next morning, Esther dropped Abigail off at Grindlewood House. Thaddeus was still resting after his ordeal. She hugged her daughter tightly and wished her good luck. Jemima let Abigail in through the side gate and Luke arrived with Trigger soon after.

'Don't tell me Jamie's still in bed,' said Luke.

'No way. He's in the fairy house with Timber,' said Jemima. 'He thinks Timber is trying to tell him something. Come on, let's see if he's found out anything.'

They ran quickly down the garden.

'Hi,' said Jamie. 'I've figured it out. Timber wants us to bring the crystal key!'

'What?' said Luke.

'Are you sure?' asked Jemima.

'Have you forgotten?' said Abigail. 'Granddad said that too.'

'I know,' said Jamie. 'But Timber was barking at the floorboards, so I took out the key. Then he picked it up in his mouth and he won't put it down.' Timber was sitting on the floor with the key sticking out of his mouth, and his paws holding it there.

'I say we bring it,' said Jamie.

'Me too,' said Abigail. 'Going west to the crones was scary but going north today could be even worse.'

'I vote yes too,' said Jemima.

They looked at each other, at Timber, at the key. They waited for Luke's vote.

'OK then,' said Luke, 'let's bring it just in case.'

'Why don't you take it, Abby?' said Jamie. 'You thought of it first.'

He took a piece of string from his coat pocket and tied the key securely before placing it around Abigail's neck. She popped it inside her sweater under her coat.

'Time to draw the circle,' said Jemima.

But Timber wouldn't budge.

When Esther returned home, she heard Thaddeus shouting upstairs. He had suddenly remembered what had been bothering him.

'Audmund! The wretch! I must tell the others!'

'Thaddeus, is that you moving about? Are you all right?' called Esther as she ran upstairs to check on him.

'Esther, it was Audmund, the augurer. It was him. I saw his ring, the one with the snake seal. I saw it on the hand that fired the spells at me. I'm certain.'

'What? Oh no!' said Esther.

'Send the nightingale ahead,' said Thaddeus. 'I'll be down in a moment.'

Esther quickly prepared him a cup of tea and sent Nura, their nightingale, off to Hollow Hill with another message for Pendrick. Thaddeus got up and got dressed as quickly as he could.

When they reached the reception chamber, Pendrick hurried over to them.

'I got your message,' he said. 'Ripley is missing. It looks like he's one of the traitors.'

'Her Majesty is distraught,' said Sparks, rushing over. 'We haven't been able to speak to her properly yet.'

'I know who the other traitor is,' said Thaddeus. 'It's Audmund. I saw his ring when he attacked me. I'm sure of it.'

'Well that explains a few things,' said Flint.

The four men went quickly to the queen's chamber. Esther waited outside.

'Your Majesty,' said Pendrick, 'the Wizard Allnutt is here and we have some more bad news, I'm afraid.'

'Audmund is the other traitor, Your Majesty,' said

Thaddeus. 'He attacked Esther and me and searched our house for *The Book of Light*.'

'One of my augurers is a traitor?' cried the queen. 'How shocking! And the book?'

'It's still safe,' said Thaddeus. He looked at the professors. 'Where are the other books?'

'They're in the vault,' said Flint.

'When did you last check them?'

'Only moments ago,' said Sparks, 'as soon as we heard Ripley was missing.'

'Check them again, and check the key too,' said Pendrick.

Sparks nodded and ran off. Suddenly there was quite a rumpus heading their way. Timber ran into the chamber, quickly followed by the children and several of the Grindlewood residents.

'What are you all doing here?' asked Esther, rushing in with them.

'It's almost seven o'clock!' cried Flint. 'You must leave at once!'

'We know,' said Jamie, 'but Timber wouldn't come into the circle unless we went down the trapdoor first.'

'We thought he wanted to tell you something,' said Jemima.

Timber trotted straight over to the queen. He spoke to her in the ancient witch language, but to the children it sounded just like barking.

'Timber asked me about a sorceress,' said the queen. 'It is true. Worfeus had a twin sister named Zora, but everyone assumed she was dead. I don't know if Bodric was her pet, but she was a very odd girl, obsessed with the dark arts, even at a young age.'

Just then, Professor Sparks burst into the chamber. 'The two parts of the WABOM are still here, safe and sound,' he said, 'and Audmund has not been seen since last night, but there's something else.'

'What is it?' said Flint.

'The gold key is missing. I can't find it anywhere.' Sparks was shaking.

Timber barked loudly at the queen.

'Timber thinks Audmund must have taken the key and then gone to warn the buzzard that you're coming for *The Book of Darkness*,' said Pendrick, turning to the children.

'Of course he has,' cried the queen. 'How did I not see this coming? How did my other augurers not see it? Lotus, tell the augurers I want to see them at once. Professors, the return of the WABOM has never been more urgent. Get to work!'

The professors and Thaddeus stood to one side and spoke quietly together.

'Audmund is very crafty,' said Thaddeus. 'He has been one step ahead of us the whole time.'

'He knows everything about us,' said Sparks. 'Everything! The WABOM, the keys …'

'But not the source of our power,' said Pendrick. 'Only the queen and the fairies know that.'

'Yes, that is a relief,' said Thaddeus.

'But if it really is Zora,' said Flint, 'we cannot let her get a hold of the keys.'

'Perhaps Audmund has a plan of his own,' said Pendrick.

'You mean Zora has a plan and Audmund has another?' asked Sparks.

'I don't know,' said Pendrick, 'but he was always secretive, sneaky and ambitious. It wouldn't surprise me one bit.'

'There could even be a third traitor,' said Thaddeus.

The others stared at him.

'They'll need someone to steal the WABOM from the vault now that Ripley and Audmund have scarpered,' said Thaddeus. 'Someone still on the inside.'

'We must triple the protection on the vault at once,' said Flint.

'How?' said Sparks. 'Our magic is all but gone.'

'Indeed it is,' said Pendrick. 'All the more reason to finish this quest quickly. Then we can renew our magic and our security.'

'This really is frightful!' said Thaddeus, looking over at the children and their pets. Timber howled loudly. It was time to go. The queen looked down at him.

'Dear Timber,' she said, 'find *The Book of Darkness* for me and save Grindlewood.'

'It's one minute to seven,' said Luke.

'Quick, draw the circle,' said Pendrick.

Abigail looked at her mother and granddad. She patted her chest where she could feel the crystal key beneath her sweater and her coat. They understood what she meant. Thaddeus nodded, and her mother tried her best to smile.

The professors moved back as Jemima drew a large circle in the middle of the queen's chamber. The brave Grindlewood Army held each other close inside the magical line. Jemima pushed in the pin at the back of the brooch and then pulled out the northern diamond. In a flash, they were gone.

⁓✿⁓

The buzzard had moved his ragged army to a new site, Bodric's Gorge. Ripley had arrived late in the night. Audmund arrived a little after him, but no one had expected the augurer to arrive with his pet dwarf-troll. They sat with Bodric and a few fat buzzards around a pile of small bones that had been stripped clean.

'Ha ha!' roared Bodric. 'The children and their dog are coming to get *The Book of Darkness*! Imagine that, *the children and their dog.*' He laughed again.

Ripley and Audmund were bored with Bodric's boasting. Grizzle, the dwarf-troll, snarled and shook his head till his horns rattled. He didn't like buzzards. They were noisy and annoying little pests. He puffed foul breath and glared at them with his one orange marble eye. The buzzards took the hint and shuffled off, and Bodric finally stopped laughing.

The hawks were just as uncomfortable as the buzzards with having a dwarf-troll in their midst.

Grizzle wasn't as large as a normal troll, but he was more than seven feet tall when he stood up straight. He looked like a big, beefy gargoyle, with the same spikey wings on his humped, hairy back and a ferocious-looking head. His sharp tusks were perhaps his scariest feature of all.

'He really is quite special, isn't he?' said Audmund, smugly. 'Trust me, you wouldn't want to annoy him too much.'

'Well, do you have *The Book of Light* yet, Audmund?' asked Bodric.

'The book is still cloaked,' replied the augurer, 'but I will have it soon.'

'And the rest?'

'The Forest Queen has two parts of the WABOM as I already told you, but it will be easy to take them from her when the Wandeleis' magic has completely faded – any day now.'

'Have you any idea where the crystal key might be?'

'It's somewhere in Grindlewood,' said Ripley.

'We already know that, you silly squirrel!' said Bodric sharply. 'A little bit of torture might reveal its whereabouts. I'll make those meddlesome children tell us where it is, and then you and your big friend here can go and get it like you were supposed to.'

Bodric risked a quick glance in Grizzle's direction. Grizzle growled and puffed smelly breath back at him.

'Quite,' said Audmund calmly. 'What have you been doing with *The Book of Darkness*, seeing as you can't read, eh, witch language?'

'I'm keeping it for Zora, of course,' said Bodric. 'I took it off some stupid Worfagons who had no idea what it was. Some of them are still here, over there.' He pointed with his wing to a bunch of warlocks who were snoring loudly. None looked as though they could muster up any magic at all. 'They were only too willing to hand over an old book for a few pieces of metal to make new swords.'

'Splendid,' said Audmund. 'And what about Zora?'

'So many questions, Audmund,' said Bodric, throwing another bone away. 'Vargon is preparing for her return and she will send me instructions herself when she is ready. All we have to do is deliver the WABOM and the gold key.'

'Which we will,' said Audmund, reaching into his pocket. 'I have it here.' He held the gold key up for a second, then put it back in his pocket before Bodric could snatch it. 'Don't worry, I will keep it safe. Now tell me, what are you hoping to get in return for such loyalty and hard work?'

'I was given the Mind-meld,' said Bodric, proudly.

'But that was some time ago,' said Audmund. 'Anything else?'

Bodric scowled. He hated how the augurer twisted everything he said. 'Zora will return and conquer all of Grindlewood to begin with. Then she will expand her kingdom far and wide,' said the buzzard. 'She will find the Wandeleis' source of power and she will reign supreme – with me by her side. That will be reward enough.'

'Oh, quite. Tell me, how … Oh hello, Festus, you're here too,' said Audmund, as the falcon landed beside them.

'Just keeping an eye on things for the mistress,' said Festus curtly. He detested Audmund and his meddling almost as much as he hated Bodric.

'Yes, everyone seems to think they are doing that,' said Audmund snidely. 'Isn't it nice that Zora has so many loyal friends to welcome her back? One wonders who her favourite might be.'

Bodric shot Audmund another angry look. Grizzle

snarled a warning back at him and Audmund smiled his sickly smile. A little further away, Ripley crunched on a nut, out of reach of all of them, but not out of earshot. The squirrel's plan was simple. He intended to get whatever he could out of this arrangement and then scarper.

Kelvin Kestrel perched on a rock nearby, pretending to be on lookout duty. He was listening carefully too, wondering which of this nasty bunch would make the best ally. Kelvin would have to choose carefully. He had always assumed that Bodric was the best choice, but after listening to that conversation, he wasn't so sure.

Chapter Twenty-two

THE BATTLE OF BODRIC'S GORGE

They had left Hollow Hill at precisely seven o'clock, but when the Grindlewood Army arrived at Bodric's Gorge it was midday. Everyone stayed absolutely quiet and still, hunkering down behind rocks and bushes. Something was wrong.

'This is another horrid place,' whispered Jemima.

'Why would they want to live in a dump like this?' asked Luke.

'Buzzards are strange,' said Jamie.

The residents were wondering about the location too. It didn't look at all like the place Oberon had described.

'I don't know where we are,' said the owl.

'Bodric must have moved,' said Timber, 'but we're in the right place. The queen said the compass wouldn't make that kind of mistake, even if its timing is a bit off.'

'If Bodric is here, the book is here,' said Gildevard.

'Stay low and quiet,' said Timber. 'We need to see what's going on before we move.'

Bodric had moved his camp to a narrow, windy gorge. Spotting intruders was easier in such a space and he knew once he had the book, interested parties would come after it.

The gorge was shaped like a huge, long snake that wound its way through the mountains, flanked on both sides by sheer rock. The wind whistled sharply, first from one end, disappearing around a bend, and then whipping back again from the other direction.

The animals were watching, listening and sniffing the air, trying to pick up important information. The birds hopped carefully among raggy branches that were growing out of cracks in the rocks. Their sharp eyes scoured the surroundings. There were few trees, only tall, sheer cliffs of rock lining the gorge. The rest of it was just rocks, boulders, spindly bushes, bleached bones and broken eggshells.

The wind had a biting chill to it and the children shivered. They watched the animals carefully, expecting

Timber to give the signal at any moment. Jemima took out the brooch. Quietly and carefully she drew a circle around where they crouched. Like the last time, it would be ready for a quick escape. She returned the brooch to one of her coat pockets. Ernie the frog was waiting patiently in the other.

Jamie checked his ring and pulled out his sword. Luke gripped his bow tightly and flexed the wire. Abigail clasped her wand, repeating her spells over and over again in her head. She checked the crystal key again. It was still there, under her sweater. Jemima crouched back beside her. Everyone was ready.

Finally, Timber gave a silent nod and the birds flew to a number of lookout posts a little further from the group. The animals waited.

'Ripley is there,' said Oberon, returning quickly. 'That augurer Audmund is there, too, with a large, hairy beast.'

'What is it?' asked Timber.

'It looks like a sort of half troll, half gargoyle. We'll have to watch that one.'

'Where did that come from?' asked Teddy.

'I think he's with the augurer,' said Spindle as

the two sparrows zoomed in. 'No one else seems to want to sit beside him.'

'His name is Grizzle,' said one of the blackbirds. 'I heard the augurer say it.'

'So Audmund has a pet beast called Grizzle,' said Timber.

'I think it's called a dwarf-troll,' said Gildevard, when he had landed. 'Don't be confused by the name. They're smaller than full trolls, but very aggressive.'

The children had spotted him too. Grizzle was bored and he began to stomp around.

'That's some troll-monster!' whispered Jemima. 'Look at him!'

'Let's hope something that big is slow and stupid,' said Luke.

'So trolls do exist!' muttered Jamie.

'All the stuff in fairy tales exists,' whispered Abigail.

'Your granddad told you, didn't he?' said Jemima. Abigail nodded. 'I knew it!'

'Right, remember the plan,' said Jamie. 'Once we have the advantage, we'll let the animals and birds take care of Bodric and his gang and we'll go after the book.'

'What about the big beasty thing?' cried Jemima.

Jamie looked at Luke, wondering if both his sword and Luke's arrows would be enough, but they didn't have time to talk about it. The kestrel had spotted them.

'Intruders!' he squawked. 'Intruders! Over there!'

'I don't believe it!' cried Gildevard. 'He's done it again!'

Audmund stood up promptly. Ripley immediately looked for somewhere to hide. Bodric turned around slowly, his head hunched between his shoulders and his beady eyes flickering with excitement.

'So they're here! The do-gooders are ready for battle.' Bodric cackled and ordered his army out. 'Attack, hawks! Attack!'

'Aren't you going to send the buzzards too?' asked Audmund.

'The hawks can take care of it,' said Bodric, spitting out a small bone. 'I'll keep my buzzards in reserve.'

Jamie climbed on top of a boulder and pulled out his sword. The approaching hawks screeched with delight.

'Oh look, a toy sword! Ha ha!'

Bodric roared with laughter. He laughed so much that he didn't see what happened next. Jamie glanced at his ring. The gold cross shone brightly in the centre of the blue stone and the sword became shiny steel. He swung it bravely as the hawks attacked. Luke fired his arrows from his position on top of another boulder. The animals leapt out from different hiding places, pulling down hawks as they flew by.

Oberon and Gildevard flew high and descended on the hawks from above. Surprised, they scattered and panicked. Many were caught and turned to dust.

Bodric frowned. 'Buzzards, get up and do your duty!' he roared at the sleepy birds beside him. 'Get up, I say!' He pecked and kicked at the buzzards till they reluctantly obeyed.

The sparrows' enchanted beaks stunned a few hawks, but they were very fast and it was hard to catch them. The blackbirds followed closely behind the sparrows, two behind Spindle and two behind Sparky. They tried to distract the hawks while the heron zoomed in, using his long sharp beak to stab them underneath. Then the garden birds lured the hawks lower to the ground, where the animals jumped out and caught them as they flew by.

The animals had little trouble dealing with the disorganised buzzards. The cats leapt off the boulders and pulled them down. Timber and Dougal jumped off the lower rocks, biting and thwacking with their paws, knocking several to the ground. Eldric and Trigger finished off any that were wounded or who hadn't taken to the air. Ramona walloped a few with her big back legs, breaking their wings or knocking them into the rock face.

After a while, a few smart hawks changed their plan and avoided these traps. Instead they split into smaller groups and zoomed around the animals to attack them from the side and from behind. They managed to stab and peck nearly all of them.

Luke called Trigger to his side. He was firing so fast he needed help collecting spent arrows. As the targets turned to dust, the arrows fell free and Trigger returned them to Luke to fire off again.

Jamie looked like a true warrior, standing on top of the rock. He slashed and swished his magical sword, knocking out buzzards and hawks alike.

Abigail cast freezing spells and wobble spells, including some at the Worfagon warlocks. They had barely woken up when the attack began, only to find their arms and legs had either frozen or turned to jelly. Only a few managed to avoid being hit, scurrying to

find shelter so they could fire a few spells of their own.

Jemima was the spotter. Her job was to see where the next attack would come from. She called out to the others as the hawks, buzzards and warlocks reorganised themselves to change their plan of attack. She kept a hand on her pocket, ready to pull Ernie out when he was needed. Luckily, there weren't any serious injuries yet, and the dwarf-troll hadn't moved. He waited beside Audmund for instructions.

'Keep an eye out for the book,' cried Timber.

'Will do,' tooted Oberon as he turned sharply and ripped two hawks that were behind him. Gildevard soared past and did the same to another two, screeching his battle cry.

On the far side of the gorge, Audmund called Grizzle and gave him some instructions. But it wasn't an order to enter the fight – not yet. Grizzle simply roared and stomped off.

The augurer moved slowly to a long narrow crack in the rock face. It was hardly noticeable from a distance, slanting back into the sheer cliff. He was more interested in the book than all this battle nonsense, and he had a good idea where it was hidden. Hopefully, Grizzle would confirm his suspicions in a moment.

Audmund looked on as Bodric's army struggled to overcome a bunch of children and garden animals. He sneered as he watched the warlocks being made fools of by a novice witch. Perhaps he could fire a few spells. After all, it wouldn't do if Bodric complained about him to Zora. He took up position behind some rocks.

The battle was hotting up. Jemima was now frantically running about with Ernie to reach the wounded. Once Audmund began casting spells, it became harder to avoid being hit. Jamie and Luke had to come down from the boulders where they were easy targets for Audmund's wand. Instead they stayed close to Jemima, trying to protect her and the frog and spot trouble before it hit them.

Abigail had to take cover as the augurer's spells grew more deadly. She was pinned down with the rabbit and fox. Bush fires were breaking out wherever there was anything to burn and lumps of rock were falling into the gorge as misdirected spells broke more chunks off the cliff face.

'We were doing fine till that augurer starting blitzing,' cried Luke.

'I know,' cried Jamie, 'and where's the troll thing?'

'Eeeek!' shrieked Jemima, dodging another one of Audmund's spells.

'Jem, get down!' cried Jamie.

Luke fired a few arrows over her head. He hit two hawks and a buzzard.

'That was cool!' cried Jamie, as he turned and sliced a couple of buzzards.

'Nice!' said Luke.

'The animals are being hit a lot,' said Jemima. 'I can't reach them fast enough.'

'I know. I hate when they get hurt,' said Jamie. 'Don't let anything happen to Ernie.'

Meanwhile, Bodric was furious. Several buzzards had been killed. Some of the really nasty ones had turned to dust. Others lay in a heap, dead or badly injured. At least a dozen had panicked and flown off. The hawks hadn't done much better, but at least none of them had deserted. Ripley wasn't anywhere to be seen. He had run to the spot where Jemima had drawn the circle, dug a small hole, squeezed in and waited. He was going to stay well clear of the danger and try and sneak a ride back to Grindlewood.

Festus and Kelvin avoided the action too. They withdrew to a nest high up in the rock face.

'We can watch them kill each other from here,' said Festus. 'That Bodric is abominable. Zora will be furious with him after this disaster.'

Kelvin looked at him but said nothing.

'I heard that remark, Festus,' said Bodric, fluttering up to their hiding place. 'How dare you! This is merely a bit of fun, entertainment. Those children and that dog will never get the book!'

'*Entertainment!*' cried Festus. 'Is that what you call it?'

Bodric sneered at the falcon and summoned a few hawks.

'Rip this falcon to pieces,' he said.

Kelvin flew out of the way just in time. The hawks pulled Festus out and tore him to shreds in mid-air.

'You can pick up his pieces afterwards,' roared the buzzard. 'Get back into battle! Now!'

Bodric looked around with his beady little eyes. The hawks were fighting bravely but it didn't look like they would win. Ripley was still out of sight. 'That sneaky little coward!' Bodric thought. Audmund was firing his wand now and again but he didn't look too bothered. 'That smug little git!' thought the buzzard. Then he remembered Grizzle. 'Where is that lump?

Argh! The book!' Bodric ignored the fighting below him and flew straight to the hiding place.

The three butterflies had accompanied the Grindlewood Army to Bodric's Gorge. Kelvin's keen eyes had spotted them earlier. He knew from Gildevard's lessons just how enchanted they could be. He flew to where he had first spotted them. 'Aha,' he thought, 'there they are!' With his eyes locked on target, he flew around several attacking hawks and headed straight for the butterflies. They were sitting quietly on a small bush, seemingly unaware of the approaching danger.

Teddy spotted the kestrel's movement and realised what was happening. 'The kestrel is after our butterflies!' he cried.

Timber raced after Teddy. The butterflies flew out of the way just in time. Teddy arrived and leapt up at the kestrel. He missed him. The brave cat turned, twisted and leapt again, clipping his wing. As Kelvin faltered, Timber lunged up and – THWACK! – knocked the kestrel to the ground.

'How could you take sides with that buzzard?' barked Timber crossly.

'I'm on no one's side but my own,' spluttered Kelvin.

'Whatever Bodric promised you is a lie,' barked the big dog. 'He's up to no good.'

'Think what you like,' said Kelvin, 'but he's not as dumb as he appears. He knows what's important.'

'Like what?' cried Teddy.

'Like whose side to be on,' said Kelvin. 'Zora is a great sorceress and hers will be the winning side. Everyone else will suffer or die.'

As Timber and Teddy thought about what to do with their prisoner, Cyril flew over.

'Is everything all right over here? Oh, you caught a kestrel.'

'This is Kelvin, Gildevard's apprentice – or he was until he changed sides,' said Timber. 'I thought we might be able to do a deal with him, but perhaps not.'

'What deal?' said the kestrel. 'You lot are done for, and it's not just Bodric or Zora you have to worry about.'

'What?' said Teddy. 'What do you mean?'

'Let's go,' said Timber. 'We'll decide what to do with him later.'

They left the kestrel where he lay. With one broken wing and the other badly bruised, he wouldn't be going anywhere. Cyril flew off and Timber and Teddy ran back to the others.

From his hole in the ground, Ripley saw and heard everything, but he didn't move.

Despite all the valiant efforts, the battle for Bodric's Gorge wasn't nearly over. Grizzle reappeared. He stood in the middle of the gorge, ready to fight at last. Audmund was over to one side, conjuring up a spell with Worfeus' wand. He called out the words and everyone stopped to see what would happen. Even Bodric turned and stared, waiting. As Audmund cried out the last word of his spell – 'metallicutius!' – everyone held their breath.

Chapter Twenty-three

THE BOOK OF DARKNESS

The hawks looked larger and meaner with their new metal cloaks. Jamie charged at the nearest one, slicing and chopping fiercely, but it was much harder to defeat them now. Luke was reloading as fast as he could and he fired off several arrows, but they couldn't penetrate the enchanted metal. He would have to aim instead for the head or neck, and that was going to be tricky.

Abigail tried to freeze the hawks, but her freezing spell didn't work on them at all. Audmund had taken care of that too. Timber jumped at every hawk within reach, trying to pull the metal off, but even with all the animals working together, it was difficult and slow.

Then they heard what they had been dreading all along.

'Attack, Grizzle, attack!' cried Audmund. 'Attack them all!'

The dwarf-troll let out an unmerciful roar and charged. He swiped and punched at everything with his huge shovel-hands and kicked with his club-sized feet.

'How on earth are we going to stop that thing?' cried Luke. 'He won't even feel these arrows.'

'Try them anyway,' cried Jamie. Luke fired six in quick succession. They stuck in Grizzle's hide like pins but didn't bother him much. Timber called the animals back behind a large boulder. The children crouched beside them, wondering what to do.

Then Jamie suddenly roared. 'No, Timber, NO!' as Timber ran straight for Grizzle. Jamie ran out after him. The other animals saw what was happening and rushed out too, but they were driven back by a huge squadron of hawks. After a few attempts, the dogs and cats managed to get through the melee, and following Timber's example, they bit and scratched Grizzle's feet and legs, hoping to make him fall over. Oberon and Gildevard swooped around his head, but the hawks were keeping them busy. Soon, everyone was back in the fight in a frantic, noisy blur.

Grizzle was belting the animals and birds about like flies. He didn't care if he hit the hawks and buzzards too, he just kept swinging his fists and stabbing his tusks. All the sparrows and blackbirds were on the ground again, in need of urgent help.

Luke and Jamie tried to protect Jemima as she ran around with Ernie again. Abigail stayed behind a boulder with the rabbits and fox, only reaching out from safety to cast more spells on buzzards and warlocks as the earlier spells wore off.

Then the heron spotted an opportunity. He flew wide and low, turning to come up behind Grizzle, over his shoulder, and then he rammed his beak into the dwarf-troll's only eye. Both howled in pain as the stabbing broke Cyril's beak and burst Grizzle's eye. The heron flew out of the way just in time to avoid Grizzle's angry fists. He managed to reach a safe spot where he waited for Ernie.

The sparrows and blackbirds were all healed, but Timber ordered them back. There would be no more action for the smaller birds. It had become too dangerous. The dogs were still struggling to slow Grizzle down, all the while fending off the attacking hawks. Timber jumped higher towards the dwarf-troll's hands, but was quickly punched away. Dougal tried to do the same and got thumped into the air. Luckily he landed on a few bushes which saved him.

The cats continued scratching and clawing at Grizzle's legs and feet, but they were easily and repeatedly shaken off. Trigger dashed in circles around him, trying to make him dizzy, but Grizzle couldn't see so he just ignored him. Timber tried one more time but was thrown against the rock face. He slid down the wall in a heap. Jamie ran to him immediately, screaming for Ernie.

'Jemima, you've got to come NOW!' roared Jamie.

'No, *you'll* be killed!' cried Luke, pulling her back.

Crossing the gorge looked almost impossible. Grizzle's injured eye was driving him crazy and he began smashing rocks in a murderous rage. On top of that, a crowd of hawks was hovering over the centre of the gorge, waiting to attack anyone who came forward.

'Luke, Jemima, come back here!' called Abigail, a few yards behind them. She took out the crystal key.

'Yes!' said Luke. 'That's it!'

He grabbed Jemima by the hand and they ran back to Abigail.

'Quick, grab it!' she cried, holding out the key.

They held it and waited for something to happen.

'Hurry up!' cried Jamie from where Timber lay on the other side of the gorge.

'Come on, come on,' said Luke, staring at the key. 'What's taking so long?'

'It'll work,' whispered Abigail. 'It has to.'

'Look, there!' squealed Jemima.

At last, the crystal key began to glow and grow, just like before.

'Hold on tight and we'll try to reach them,' said Luke. 'Ready? Move!'

The key shone brightly, covering the three children with its shield of protective light. They moved as quickly as they could, being careful not to let go of the key, across the narrow gorge to Jamie and Timber. When they reached them, Jamie grabbed a hold of the key to expand the shield to cover him and Timber too. Jemima lifted Ernie out and put him on Timber's side as they huddled over the injured dog. But suddenly the key began to fade.

'What's going on?' cried Jamie. 'Why is it stopping?'

'Maybe Audmund is doing something,' said Jemima, trying to see where the augurer was.

'Or the magic is weakening, like all the Wandeleis' magic,' said Abigail.

'Not now, not now,' cried Jamie.

When the light went out, Abigail put the key away. Timber was on his feet again and together they ran for cover behind some rocks. Oberon and Gildevard swooped in to land beside them.

'Timber, we think there's an opening behind the rock face a little bit further down the gorge,' said Oberon.

'We saw Grizzle disappear down there earlier so there must be a way in,' said Gildevard.

'The book could be in there,' said Timber. 'Check it out, but be careful.'

Oberon and Gildevard flew off.

'No more fighting, Timber,' said Jamie. 'We've got to find the book. Then we're leaving.'

Timber barked a few times and dragged his paws along the ground. He looked over towards the rock face, lifting his muzzle up and down, pointing.

'No, Timber,' said Jamie, a little confused. 'We can't fight Grizzle – he's too big. We're staying here till we figure out where the book might be.'

'Jamie, I think the owl and eagle know where it is,' said Jemima.

They risked a peek over the boulder and saw the owl and eagle flying further down the gorge, close to the rock face.

'Either that, or they're leaving us,' said Jamie. 'Let's follow them.'

'We'll have to use a gemstone,' said Abigail.

'What?' said Luke.

'She's right,' said Jamie. 'The key has faded and we have to get past Grizzle and Audmund to get down there.'

'Yeah, you're right,' said Luke. He popped out the ruby. Then BANG!

Something hit Luke. He was knocked sideways and the gemstone fell out of his hand.

'No, no, no!' cried Jamie.

Grizzle had thrown another rock and it hit Luke on the arm. The ruby rolled out of reach.

'Did you finish the wish?' cried Jamie.

'I didn't even start,' said Luke. 'Crikey, that hurt!'

'Are you all right?' asked Jemima. The others looked at him anxiously.

'Sort of,' said Luke, holding his arm awkwardly.

'We have to get that ruby!' cried Jamie.

Going after the ruby would mean the ever-increasing flock of metal hawks and a very angry dwarf-troll would see them. Even Timber hesitated, knowing Jamie would follow him if he ran out again.

'Oh, this is bad,' said Jemima. 'We have to use the ruby next.'

Help came quickly from an unlikely source. Benny, the buckled old buzzard, and a few of his pals snuck around them from behind. The dogs smelled them and growled, ready to pounce.

'Look out! More buzzards!' cried Abigail.

'I'll get them,' said Jamie. He raised his sword, but Timber noticed something. He barked and then Jamie saw what it was. 'That buzzard has the ruby!'

Sure enough, Benny held the ruby in his beak. He scuttled over to Timber and dropped it on the ground in front of him. 'Oh! Thanks,' said Jamie, reaching over and picking it up. Benny just looked at him with his sad, old eyes and then shuffled away. The other buzzards followed him.

'Let's try it again,' said Jamie, returning to the others.

'You do it this time,' said Luke. Jemima was helping

him to sit still, while Abigail was attempting her first Bone-mending spell.

Jamie closed his fist and his eyes. He had to concentrate hard. He thought only of what they needed – help. The stone disappeared. For a few moments there was nothing, just a lot of squawking as Benny and his friends were punished by Bodric and the hawks.

'Is anything happening?' asked Luke.

'It will. It has to,' said Jemima.

'Crikey, I hope I didn't mess up,' muttered Jamie. 'The animals and birds have suffered enough and we still have to get the book. Where's the magic? Come on!'

Timber called the other animals and birds together.

'Teddy, keep everyone together and stay out of sight,' said Timber. 'We're going after the book.'

'We'll tuck in under these rocks,' said Teddy. 'We should be safe from attack here.'

'Good. Come quickly with the others when I bark,' said Timber. 'Trigger, Dougal, get ready to come with me.'

The hawks were regrouping and preparing to strike. Grizzle let out a terrifying roar and pounded his fists on the ground. It felt like an earthquake as the ground shuddered and more rubble fell from the rock face. He was just about to charge on all fours when a strange noise came from further down the gorge. It was the sound of wings flapping, huge wings, and it kept getting louder. Then there was a hissing sound and then another sound, more like thunder this time. Everyone turned to look as the noises grew louder.

'Something's happening,' said Jamie.

'I hope it's something good,' said Luke nervously.

It was extraordinary.

Three fire-breathing dragons with wide rainbow wings swooped into Bodric's Gorge. Chloe, Calista and Celeste, the three Grindlewood butterflies, had transformed once again. This time they had long spiked tails, tough dragon hide, large teeth and fire power.

'Look, we've got dragons!' cried Jamie.

Grizzle roared at what he could only hear and smell, and Bodric's army screeched in terror. The Grindlewood dragons gushed plumes of fire at the hawks, heating up their metal coats. Some were roasted inside the red hot metal and others fell from the sky as the metal buckled and pierced their wings.

'This is our chance,' said Jamie. 'The dragons will

take care of Grizzle and the hawks.'

'Watch for a gap,' said Luke. 'We don't want to get caught in the middle of all this mayhem.'

As they watched the dragons take up the fight, the children wanted to run but were afraid of being hit by dragon fire, falling burning hawks or Grizzle's missiles. After a few minutes, Timber prodded Jamie firmly with his nose and barked.

'He's right. We should go now,' said Jamie.

They scrambled up and ran. Timber, Dougal and Trigger raced along the rock face, ducking left and right as more burning birds fell out of the sky. The children hurried after them. The flashing gold cross on Jamie's ring shone brightly, and it caught Audmund's eye; so too did Abigail's wand.

'So the children don't just have a big, brave dog; they have the crystal key, Wanda's wand, Gorlan's ring – and now dragons,' said Audmund. 'Impressive, but they're still no match for me.'

He raised his wand and fired a spell directly at them, but one of the dragons flew across to block it. Chloe was hit. She fell straight down, landing near the children with a loud thump. Gildevard and Oberon screeched overhead and circled down.

'Keep going. The entrance is just ahead,' cried Gildevard.

'Meet us there,' barked Timber, 'and don't touch Bodric. I want to talk to him.'

The dogs ran ahead of the children. They tried to hurry, but there was always something to dodge or avoid, slowing them down.

Luckily, Grizzle was kept busy trying to fend off the dragons. Metal hawks were still melting and falling out of the sky, but most of the buzzards had snuck away and the few that remained were no match for Calista and Celeste.

The augurer took aim again. 'CRACK!' The second killing spell hit its target. Calista fell to the ground, taking a few hawks with her on the way down.

'Two down,' said Audmund to himself. 'Grizzle can take care of the third. Time for me to get the book.'

From the outside, it looked like a high, narrow passage into the mountain. Near the ground and behind a wall of rock, the crack was quite wide and it opened out wider still. Even Grizzle had managed to squeeze in on all fours and then stand up in the cave-like space inside. The dogs had no difficulty getting in. Gildevard flew in at the highest and narrowest point.

Oberon followed. Their shrieks echoed eerily inside the rocky cavern.

'It's up here!' cried the eagle, soaring above the dogs. *The Book of Darkness* was in a niche in the wall near the top of the crevice. Bodric was already there, with a handful of buzzards who had been hiding.

'Stay back!' cried Bodric.

Gildevard and Oberon eyed each other and flew straight for the book, knocking it from the ledge. As it fell to the ground, it knocked out two buzzards and scared off another two. Bodric flew after it. Oberon and Gildevard went after him and they all came to a sudden stop where the book lay, on the ground in front of Timber. He placed a paw on the book, lowered his head and growled.

Suddenly Audmund emerged from the shadows, his wand raised. But once again help came from an unexpected source. Bodric turned on the augurer. He knew he had probably lost the book, but he wasn't going to lose Worfeus' wand. He flew straight into the augurer's face, pecking and clawing, determined to get it off him. 'Give me that wand,' he screeched. 'Worfeus' wand is mine. I found it. Give it to me!'

'No, it's mine now,' cried Audmund. 'Ripley found it and gave it to *me*.'

'I told Ripley where he could find it. That makes it mine!' cried Bodric.

'It's *mine*!'

'No, it's *mine*.'

The augurer and the buzzard continued their wrestling.

Outside, the children were blocked by Grizzle. He was so wild with rage that they couldn't risk running around him.

'Timber's barking for us,' said Jamie. 'We have to get past.'

'Try the key again,' said Jemima.

'Will it work?' asked Luke.

'I wish I knew,' said Abigail, taking it out.

They each grabbed hold of it. Luckily, it increased in size immediately and the light appeared quicker this time too. The protective light surrounded them as they moved slowly towards the crevice. Grizzle stopped roaring. He listened and then he heard them. He groped around for another rock and threw it in their direction. It bounced right off the light.

'It works!' squealed Jemima.

'I guess that means we're still worthy,' said Luke.

'Hurry,' said Jamie. 'Timber's still barking.'

They moved quicker and quicker until the temptation to run was too great. They had only run a few yards when Jemima tripped, lost her grip on the key and tumbled to the ground. Grizzle heard her fall and stomped in her direction, kicking everything in front of him. She shrieked, which only told him exactly where she was. Luke and Abigail were a little ahead before they realised what had happened.

'Get the book!' cried Jamie, turning back to Jemima. He whooshed his sister up and they scrambled out of the way just in time to avoid Grizzle's swinging punch. Jemima stopped suddenly, tugging Jamie back.

'The brooch!' she screamed. 'It fell out of my pocket.'

'What? How?' cried Jamie, and then they heard it.

CRUNCH! Grizzle smashed the brooch under his enormous foot. A little red puff of smoke was all that was left.

'NO!' screamed Jemima.

Jamie looked up at Celeste, the last butterfly dragon. She swooped in closer to Grizzle, drawing his attention away from them. Jamie grabbed Jemima's hand and they ran for their lives. When they reached the rock face, Abigail and Luke pulled them inside.

Outside, brave Celeste had gone too close to Grizzle's angry fists. He grabbed her tail and walloped her into the cliff. She was gone.

The children caught their breath and looked around. Timber was barking. The owl and the eagle were screeching and circling, keeping any stray buzzards away. Over to the side, Bodric and Audmund were still squabbling over Worfeus' wand. Suddenly, there was a loud CRACK!, then a BANG!, followed by a flash, and both the buzzard and the augurer vanished.

'What the …? Crikey!' said Jamie. 'Where did they go?'

'Magic took them away,' whispered Abigail. 'Someone else's magic.'

'What? Whose?' asked Jemima.

'I've no idea, but it wasn't me.'

'Quick, grab the book,' said Luke. 'Magic might bring them back again.'

Jamie picked up *The Book of Darkness*, a worn black book with its title written in blood-red. It was much thinner than *The Book of Wisdom*, but almost as heavy and it had a bitter smell.

'Time to go,' said Jamie, clutching the book tightly.

Timber trotted over to the entrance. He barked to call the others. They arrived quickly as Grizzle sat on his hunkers, moaning and nursing his eye. The hawks had more or less given up.

'Forget the other circle,' said Luke. 'It'll be quicker if we leave from in here.'

'I, I, em, I dropped the brooch,' said Jemima, gulping nervously. 'How will we get home?'

For a few seconds, they all felt their tummies churn as panic gripped them.

'We have one more gemstone, don't we?' said Jamie, looking at Luke.

'Yes! Yes, we do,' said Luke, looking at his wrist, 'just the one.'

'Oh, whew!' said Jemima.

'We need something to draw the circle,' said Luke.

'Use your sword, Jamie,' cried Abigail.

'Good idea.'

The animals and birds huddled close to the children as Jamie drew the magical line. 'Right, let's ask the gemstone to take us home.'

They looked anxiously at each other.

'I really hope it can do what the brooch did,' said Jemima.

Outside, Grizzle was roaring again. Timber howled back at him, as Jamie pressed out the last gemstone. It was a diamond. 'We needed them all,' he said, looking at it sparkle, 'every last one.'

'That was close,' said Luke, 'very close.'

Jamie held the stone, closed his eyes and wished them safely back to Grindlewood. With a flash of lightning and a loud roll of thunder, they were gone.

Grizzle stomped around Bodric's Gorge for days, hungry, angry and sore. Ripley was still waiting at the circle where the Grindlewood Army had arrived earlier in the day. By the following morning he realised that he had a very long walk home. Kelvin Kestrel was left to his fate. Like Festus, he became supper for the metal hawks who had survived the battle of the gorge. Bodric and Audmund were … elsewhere.

Chapter Twenty-four

THE RENEWAL CHARM

On 30 October at 7.30 p.m., Timber led the children down the tunnel to Hollow Hill. They met up with Thaddeus and Esther on the way. Exhausted, relieved and happy, the four children followed Timber into the queen's chamber to return the final two parts of the WABOM and the crystal key. Esther and Thaddeus walked proudly behind them – but quite a lot had happened while the Grindlewood Army was away.

For days, the three professors had been poring over *The Book of Potions and Spells* and *The Book of Wisdom*. After several attempts, they finally perfected a spell to remove the tree curse. The tree broke apart and fell away with loud creaks and groans. The queen emerged in tatters and fell to the ground. Her fairies rushed to assist her. A few hours later, Queen Lyra came out of her private quarters, looking a little refreshed.

'Oh, Your Majesty, this is wonderful!' cried Sparks.

'How do you feel, Your Majesty?' asked Flint.

'I'm fine, thank you, gentlemen,' said the queen. 'I'm a bit stiff and sore, but I always knew you would free me in the end. Well done, all of you. Now, what of Timber and the children?'

'They are on their way here now, Your Majesty,' said Pendrick.

'And the book?' asked the queen.

'They have *The Book of Darkness*,' replied Pendrick, 'and they will also be bringing *The Book of Light*.'

'At last,' said the queen. 'Lock up the WABOM in the vault, Pendrick. I will perform the Renewal Charm at dawn tomorrow, Halloween morning. Make sure the children and their pets attend, especially Timber.'

'Of course,' said Pendrick, 'and welcome back, Your Majesty.'

'We have no word yet on the gold key,' said Sparks.

'Fortunately, we don't need it for the Renewal Charm,' said the queen, 'but it will be our next task. Now, gentlemen, send out the messengers with the good news.'

Sparks and Flint hurried off. Pendrick stayed

behind. The queen knew what concerned him.

'Worry not, Pendrick, I have chosen a successor,' said the queen, 'and I will be needing *The Book of Light.*'

'Oh, I see,' said Pendrick. 'I will make the necessary arrangements.'

He left the queen and caught up with Flint and Sparks in one of the tunnels.

'Oh good heavens,' said Flint. '*The Book of Light*?'

'That hasn't been done in a thousand years,' gasped Sparks. 'Did she say who?'

'No,' said Pendrick, 'but it's not hard to guess.'

The professors nodded knowingly to each other and then went about their duties.

When Timber and the children arrived, they were greeted warmly.

'At last the WABOM is whole again. Thank you,' said Sparks.

'And the crystal key!' cried Flint. 'Thank you children, animals, birds. Yes, all of you, thank you!'

Flint and Sparks took the WABOM and the key away to the vault, the deepest and most enchanted chamber in Hollow Hill.

'We owe you a great deal,' said Pendrick. 'Wanda

was right about all of you, and so was Her Majesty.'

Timber barked and then gave a little howl.

'And especially you, Timber,' said Pendrick, stroking the dog's ears.

'She hasn't forgotten about the collar, has she?' asked Jamie.

'Of course not,' said Pendrick. 'It will be removed during the ceremonies tomorrow.'

'Tomorrow? But Professor!'

'Don't worry, Jamie. Timber will be free. I promise,' said Pendrick. 'The queen can't do it right now. She has been resting since we reversed the tree curse.'

'You did it?' cried Esther. 'That's wonderful!'

'Congratulations!' said Thaddeus.

'We all did it. You and Esther, too,' said the professor.

'Well, this is cause for celebration,' said Thaddeus.

'Indeed it is,' said Pendrick. 'Her Majesty would like all of you to join us for the ceremonies tomorrow, including the Renewal Charm at dawn.'

'Wonderful!' said Thaddeus. 'That is such an honour,' he said, turning to the children.

'And all of the pets too,' said Pendrick. 'And there's one more thing.'

'Oh?' said Thaddeus.

'The queen will be using *The Book of Light*,' said Pendrick.

'Oh, I see,' said Thaddeus, glancing at Esther.

The professors said goodbye, as they had a lot to prepare for the next day. Timber led the way home as usual, howling in celebration most of the way. Thaddeus was totally bamboozled by all the children's questions about the ceremonies. Each answer he gave seemed to raise even more questions. The tunnels echoed with all their noise and chatter. Everyone was so excited. Everyone except Esther. She remained in a world of her own.

They stopped when they came to where the tunnel split into three.

'Listen up, everyone,' said Thaddeus. 'The Renewal Charm is a very solemn ceremony. Everyone must be on their best behaviour.'

'We understand, Mr Allnutt,' said Jemima, bouncing on her toes with excitement.

'Very good, and I'm sure Timber will tell his garden friends to do the same, won't you, Timber?' Timber licked Thaddeus' hand. 'Excellent!' said the wizard. 'It'll be an early start, so make sure you all get a good night's sleep. We'll meet here at six o'clock sharp, OK?'

'Six?' said Luke. 'I thought it was at dawn, a little after seven.'

'A lot has to happen before the Renewal Charm, so don't be late!' said Thaddeus.

'We'll be on time,' said Jamie.

The Allnutts waved goodnight and took the tunnel to their house in the village. Timber led the others down the centre tunnel and back to the fairy house. It was going to be the most exciting Halloween ever.

The Grindlewood Army arrived to a packed chamber. The walls were brightly decorated with candles and flowers and stars sparkled from the chamber ceiling. Pendrick showed the pets to the front, where they all sat or perched in a remarkably orderly way. The children, Thaddeus and Esther stood right behind them.

Everyone bowed when the queen entered. She wore exquisite robes of green and gold silk and on her head was the sparkling Tiara Lei. Despite her long ordeal living as a tree, the queen looked calm and beautiful. She stood in front of her throne.

'Good morning, friends. Before we begin our celebration breakfast, I must thank the children and their pets for making this day possible.' She turned to them. 'Children and residents of Grindlewood, what you did was truly astonishing. Thank you all from the bottom of my heart.'

The chamber erupted in cheers, whistles and shouts. When they quietened down, the queen continued, 'Timber, I have a promise to keep.'

Timber trotted forward. The queen chanted briefly and waved her wand. Cordelia's Collar popped open. Lotus removed it and returned it to its glass case. 'You are free again, brave Timber.' Timber shook his head, gave a little 'thank you' bark and trotted back to his place in front of Jamie.

'Good boy, Timber, good boy,' said Jamie as he hugged his dog.

The children smiled and giggled as everyone clapped and cheered again. The queen raised her hand for quiet.

'I must also thank my loyal professors, Pendrick, Flint and Sparks, who tirelessly worked to free me from the tree curse. As you can see, with the help of the returned WABOM, they finally succeeded.'

The queen smiled warmly and the Wandeleis broke into loud applause. A few firecrackers went off over their heads.

'I also must thank our dear returned friend, the Wizard Allnutt, for his loyalty, sacrifice and hard work. I would like to welcome him back and promote him to the position of professor.' Thaddeus beamed with pride. 'Come forward please, Professor Allnutt, to receive your seal.' Everyone cheered as Thaddeus stepped forward and bowed. The queen handed him the special seal of office, a five-sided silver coin with the Wandeleis' symbol, a lily, etched on it.

'Congratulations, Thaddeus! Congratulations!' shouted the professors.

'Thank you, Your Majesty. Thank you, everyone,' said Thaddeus and he returned to his place.

'As you know,' continued the queen, 'we will be performing the Renewal Charm at sunrise. One of my fairies is overground now, waiting to let us know the precise moment of the dawn. Afterwards I will announce my successor. But now it is time to celebrate and feast!'

She waved her wand in a wide arc and the whole chamber filled with chairs, tables and plates piled high with food. Trays of drinks floated around so everyone could take whatever they liked. There were even treats for the animals and birds.

Everyone sat down to eat and to chatter. They laughed and joked about the quest. Now that it was over, they didn't really remember all the scary bits, just the excitement and the wonderment of all the magic they had seen and learned.

After about an hour or so, a fairy ran into the chamber and everyone hushed. The sun was just breaking the horizon. It was time for the Renewal Charm.

With a wave of their wands, the professors cleared away the feast and took their positions beside the queen. The fairies and augurers, minus Audmund, stood on the other side of the throne. The four parts of the WABOM and the crystal key were placed on a table in front of the queen. She took the key in her hand and addressed the chamber. 'This is the last time that I will use this wonderful enchanted key,' she said. 'I must tell you that some pages are missing from *The Book of Darkness* and from *The Book of Potions and Spells*. This means that the renewal of our magic may not be perfect, but we will proceed with the ceremony, as it is so long overdue.'

All the Wandeleis bent their heads, folded their arms and closed their eyes. The queen placed the four parts of the WABOM together, one on top of the other. She spoke for a few minutes in an ancient tongue and everyone waited. A whistle of wind blew into the chamber from nowhere. It whipped around the four books, binding them like an invisible string.

The queen placed the crystal key on top of the WABOM and it melted into the old leather. She chanted another spell and a pillar of blue light burst from the WABOM, up to the ceiling, and then spread all around the chamber. No one moved or made a sound. The children and their pets watched in awe.

After a few minutes the light faded and then disappeared. The key reformed and appeared on top of the cover, whole again. The queen handed it to Lotus, who placed it on a tiny velvet cushion. The WABOM separated into its four parts and the queen placed them side by side on the table. The Wandeleis opened their eyes and breathed in the magic.

Chapter Twenty-five

A NEW QUEEN

The queen had a few more things to say before naming her successor.

'My people,' she said, 'for most of my reign, we suffered terribly at the hands of the warmongering Worfagons. Today, we have a new enemy. Audmund and the squirrel have been outlawed because together they were plotting to steal the WABOM, and unfortunately they have stolen our gold key. We believe that they are assisting the return of the sorceress, Zora, whom we suspect has evil plans of her own.'

There were shrieks and cries from the audience.

'I think there might be another quest, you know,' whispered Luke.

'Sounds like it,' said Jamie.

The others looked at him. The animals were thinking the same thing.

'We're not finished with Worfeus after all,' growled Timber.

'Not if his sister is anything like him,' said Teddy.

They all quietened down, as the queen was about to name her successor.

'I have chosen Wanda Willow to be your new queen.'

The announcement came as quite a shock. Wanda had been dead for more than six years. There was a lot of shuffling and muttering as the queen held up *The Book of Light*.

'It is many years since this book was used to bring anyone back from the dead, but I believe this is Wanda's destiny. I will now call on the Lord and Lady of the Light to return Wanda to us as Queen of the Wandeleis ... and to take me in her place, as is the rule.'

The audience was stunned. The queen sat on her throne while the professors asked the audience to make a space in the centre of the chamber. The fairies placed lilies and laurel leaves on the table around *The Book of Light* and formed a large garland on the ground. Scented candles were lit around the room. Everyone waited.

The queen stood up. The professors, including Thaddeus, stood at her side as she opened *The Book of Light* to chapter five. The children stood perfectly still, their hearts racing. They could hardly believe what they were seeing and hearing. The animals and birds didn't move or make a sound. No one did.

Lotus turned the pages silently as the queen sang the incantation. The professors chanted quietly in the background. The candles flickered, burning quickly to the end of their wicks. By the time the queen was finished, it was pitch dark.

Suddenly, a shocking white light appeared in the middle of the chamber. As it calmed, two tall and elegant figures stepped from it – the Lord and Lady of the Light. Everyone took a sharp breath and bowed. The children did likewise. Even the animals bent down, tucking their heads under their paws, and the birds tucked their beaks into their feathers.

Dressed in flowing white robes embroidered with gold, the spirits illuminated the chamber. A gentle peace fell on the room as the Ancients stood before their astounded audience. The queen bowed before them.

'You have called us from the farthest sun, Queen Lyra,' said Lord Larius in a strong, echoing voice. 'What is your wish?'

'My Lord,' said the queen, rising slowly, 'I wish for you to return Wanda Willow as our new queen. I offer you myself in exchange.'

'You are a brave and noble queen, Lyra,' said Lady Leilandra in her soft, sweet tones. 'We have seen your suffering.'

'But you have earned our respect and our favour,' said Lord Larius. 'You have chosen well, so we will grant your wish.'

The Lord and Lady of the Light moved their hands over Queen Lyra and for a few moments she returned to her youth and extraordinary beauty. She thanked her people for their friendship and loyalty. She shook hands with the professors, Esther, and Thaddeus.

'Oh, Your Majesty,' said Esther, almost weeping, 'thank you for bringing my sister back.'

'Wanda was always my choice,' said the queen. 'Serve her well.'

'We will,' said Thaddeus.

'And to you children, Timber, and friends,' said the queen. 'Thank you for protecting Grindlewood with all your hearts and for coming to our aid when we needed you.' She patted Timber on the head one last time. 'Perhaps one day Queen Wanda will tell you some more of Grindlewood's secrets.'

'Em, Your Majesty,' said Jamie. 'I think Timber always knew you didn't mean him any harm, but I was terrified I would lose him. I –'

'Jamie, it is you who must forgive me,' said the queen. 'Take good care of Timber. He is very special.'

Jamie nodded. He found it hard to look at her.

The chamber was full of whispering, sobbing and sniffling. Suddenly the white flames blazed again and Wanda stepped out of the bright white light. Queen Lyra embraced her and gave her her final instructions. The queen's youth and beauty began to fade, a sign that it was time for her to go. She handed Wanda her regal wand and placed the Tiara Lei on the new queen.

'Rule well, Queen Wanda.'

The old queen walked over to the Lord and Lady of the Light. Together they stepped into the white light, and then they were gone. The room returned to darkness.

The candles slowly relit around the chamber and Timber howled. Everyone stared at their new, young queen. She was breathtakingly beautiful, with deep-green eyes, rosebud lips, shiny black hair and milky-white skin.

'My people,' said Queen Wanda. 'I am honoured to have been chosen. Queen Lyra has asked me to begin my reign by honouring our Grindlewood friends. Timber, please come forward.'

The malamute trotted over to the new queen.

'Dear, brave Timber,' she said, 'you truly are the bravest dog in the world. Like Queen Lyra, I have no doubt that you must be descended from Tyrus, one of the greatest heroes from our past. You will retain the gift of the ancient witch tongue, which I am sure you will find useful on your adventures.' The queen waved her wand over Timber's head. He barked and then he trotted back to Jamie.

'Now, let me see Ernie,' said the queen.

Jemima walked nervously forward. She took the frog out of her pocket. He looked up at the queen, bewildered, his eyes bulging bigger than ever.

 'Ernie, you will keep your healing powers.' She waved her wand and uttered a few ancient witch words. The frog kept staring at her and then said, 'Ribbit.'

Jemima popped him back in her pocket.

'Jamie, Abigail and Luke, come and stand beside Jemima.' She turned to Jamie first. 'You may keep Gorlan's ring, Jamie. You have earned it for your bravery. In time, you may earn Gorlan's sword and shield too.'

'Thank you very much,' said Jamie, feeling very proud. He wondered for a moment what he would have to do to earn a magical sword and shield.

The queen turned to Luke next. 'Luke, take this bow and these arrows. They once belonged to Hector, our greatest archer from the golden age. You have earned them.' A young wizard handed them to Luke.

'Um, thank you, Wanda. I mean, Your Majesty,' said Luke. The queen smiled at him, remembering the shy little boy she had met seven years ago in Grindlewood Forest.

'Do you still have the empty String of Charms?' asked Wanda. Luke had it in his pocket and he handed it to the queen. She held it in her hand, waved her wand and a small velvet pouch appeared in its place. She gave it to Jemima. 'I have heard that you are a true believer, Jemima.'

'I've always believed in magic, Your Majesty,' said Jemima.

'You will be the keeper of these gems, Queen Lyra's Gems. As ever, you must truly believe in their power to receive your wish.'

'Thank you, Your Majesty,' whispered Jemima, nervously taking the pouch. She peeped in and saw seven coloured stones.

'Abigail, my niece and our newest witch – congratulations,' said the queen, embracing her. The audience clapped.

Abigail smiled at her but she was very nervous. She had been waiting to own up to something and it just burst out. 'Your Majesty, em, Aunt Wanda, em, I've been using your wand. I'm so sorry. I didn't know you were coming back, and ...' Abigail held out the wand, thinking she was in a lot of trouble.

'That wand is no longer mine, Abigail,' said the queen gently. 'It chose you as its new owner. It is yours for as long as you wish.' Abigail was so relieved she nearly swooned. 'I would like you to continue your training here in Hollow Hill with our special teachers, fairies Elva and Spira.'

Abigail almost screamed, and so did Jemima.

Thaddeus had told them about the two famous fairies and what a privilege it would be to be taught by them.

'You will also be the guardian of a new compass brooch, one that will replace the Brooch of Balmedoch,' said the queen. 'The professors are already working on it and I hear they have a few improvements in mind.'

'Yes, Your Majesty,' said Sparks. 'One or two alterations to the time changes are required as they posed some problems for –'

'It will be ready soon, Your Majesty,' interrupted Pendrick.

'Thank you, gentlemen. Abigail,' said the queen quietly, 'I know the Tiara Lei fits you. You are therefore a potential future queen. This is something you should be proud of. But for now enjoy your lessons and do not worry about the future. It will take care of itself.' The queen smiled at her, but Abigail was feeling woozy again. Jamie put his arm around her to steady her, hoping she wouldn't faint in front of everyone.

'Oh, thanks, Jamie,' said Abigail, weakly.

'Eh, sure,' said Jamie. 'Are you OK now?'

Abigail just looked at him. Jamie took his arm away, suddenly noticing how like her aunt she was. Esther brushed past to reach her sister, tears running down her face.

'Queen Wanda! I can hardly believe it!' she said.

The two sisters embraced.

'We've a lot to talk about, Esther,' said Wanda. 'I'll send for you soon.'

Esther nodded and wiped away a few tears. Wanda turned to leave, her fairies fluttering around her.

'The queen is about to go,' said Jemima, nudging Jamie back to reality. Everyone stood and bowed as the queen left the chamber. The Wandeleis went back to their duties and Timber howled his celebratory howl – the biggest, longest, happiest howl he could muster. It was time to go home, and almost time for the party!

Chapter Twenty-six

WARNING SKY

After such a big breakfast, no one really thought about lunch, and by mid-afternoon preparations for the double birthday-Halloween party were well under way.

While the children were busy on the quest, their mums had made lovely Halloween costumes for them. There were shrieks of delight from the girls, and cries of 'Cool!' and 'Brilliant!' from the boys when they saw what was hanging in Jamie and Jemima's bedrooms.

Jamie was a medieval knight, complete with a (wobbly) silver (plastic) sword. Luke was Robin Hood. His outfit came with a fun set of bow and arrows. Jemima and Abigail were going to dress up as witches, with long capes – one purple, one green – tall peaked hats and two star-studded, sparkly (fake) wands.

'Wow, thanks Mum and Mrs Allnutt and Mrs Finlay,' said Jemima.

'You're welcome, dear,' said Gloria. 'Now don't be too long getting ready. Your friends will be arriving soon.'

The mums went downstairs to check on the preparations in the kitchen. Out in the garden, Greg had safely covered up the large hole beside the well. He joined Arthur and Thaddeus who were checking to see the marquee was OK, the outdoor heaters were working and that Thaddeus' large assortment of magic tricks was ready.

'Are you all set for the performance then, Thaddeus?' asked Greg.

'Oh yes,' said Thaddeus. 'I'm looking forward to it.'

'No explosions, I hope,' said Arthur, grinning.

'No, nothing like that, just pure magic,' said Thaddeus, his eyes twinkling with merriment.

The party really was fantastic. The treasure hunt around the huge garden was hilarious and frantic, and even the pets joined in. Afterwards, all the children piled into Greg and Arthur's trucks and they went trick-or-treating around the village. They returned to the house laden with goodies.

Thaddeus played the role of magician for the evening. He told exciting tales of witches, warlocks, magic and spells and then he performed some amazing tricks. The children thought he was brilliant and even the adults were impressed. The party finished up with a lovely supper and a huge chocolate birthday cake for the two girls.

Luke and Abigail stayed on longer than everyone else, mostly because they always did, but also because their parents were still chatting in the house.

'You had us all convinced with your magic, Thaddeus,' said Greg. 'That really was a superb show!'

'Thank you Greg, I've had a lot of practice over the years,' said Thaddeus.

'It's been a great end to a hectic week!' said Gloria.

'Yes, I can't believe how quickly this week has gone by,' said Alice. 'I've hardly seen Luke over the mid-term break, and what with getting ready for the party, time has really flown. The children are back to school on Monday.'

'It certainly was an exciting time!' said Esther. 'Thank you so much for having the party in your garden. It's such a special place.'

Outside, the children watched the animals and

birds gather for their final chat of the day.

'I always knew that Timber was the bravest dog in the world,' said Jamie, 'but now it's official. Even the magical people agree.'

'He is a super dog, a super-mal,' said Luke, 'but we can't forget the others, can we?'

'You're right,' said Jamie, 'they were all fantastic. What a great little army we have.'

'That's for sure,' said Luke as he tried to shoot a plastic arrow. It flopped to the ground. Dougal picked it up and decided it would be good for chewing.

'Are you OK, Abby?' asked Jamie. 'I mean, about everything?'

'I'm getting used to it,' said Abigail.

'I think you're really lucky,' said Jemima. 'I'd love to be a witch.'

Oberon tooted before flying off to hunt. As they watched him disappear over the trees, the children noticed the strange evening sky.

'Why is the sky so red tonight?' asked Jamie.

'Yeah, sunset was hours ago,' said Luke.

'I think it looks angry,' said Abigail.

The others looked at her. She was doing it again,

saying things that sounded strange but important, out of the blue.

'We only have one day left before the break is over,' said Luke, changing the subject. 'Then it's back to all the usual stuff.'

'I wonder how long the usual stuff will last,' said Jamie.

The animals and birds were talking about some of the same things.

'Well, that was a really special day,' said Timber.

'It certainly was,' said Dougal, licking custard off his nose.

'Do you mean the quest, the old queen, the new queen or the party?' asked Norville.

'Good question, my prickly friend!' said Eldric.

'The quest,' said Teddy.

'Surely you mean the two queens,' purred Sylvie.

'I thought you meant the party, and that custard pie!' said Dougal.

'Did I miss something?' asked the Brigadier, having just woken up from another snooze after a bellyful of jelly and ice cream.

'Timber is officially the bravest dog in the world,' said Teddy proudly.

'Didn't we know that already?' said the Brigadier.

'I am no braver than anyone else,' said Timber modestly.

'Yes you are,' said Teddy. 'We all think so.'

'Thank goodness we didn't have any battles in the garden this time,' said Norville.

'That would have been outrageous!' said the Brigadier, 'but we would have sorted it out, ahem, wouldn't we, Sylvie?'

'Of course, Brigadier, just like we always used to,' said Sylvie.

'Isn't it funny,' said Timber, 'how Grindlewood's secrets keep revealing more mysteries, troubles, and then –'

'And then more quests?' said Oberon.

'Yes,' said Timber. 'We really don't know what will happen next.'

'I see Gildevard didn't stay for the party,' said Norville.

'It's always hard to know whose side he's on, isn't it?' said Teddy.

'Gildevard is on his own side,' said Timber, 'and whenever we ask for his help, we must remember that.'

'Has anyone else noticed the sky?' asked Dougal.

'I've never seen it like that before,' said Cindy. The others looked up.

'I hope it's not a warning,' muttered Timber, mostly to himself, but Teddy heard him.

'Well, good night everyone and sleep well,' said the Brigadier, and he trotted off to the kennel. The others headed off too.

Timber, Teddy and Dougal did the final patrol. Before they turned in, Timber howled loudly to remind everyone in Grindlewood that he was their protector for as long as he lived. The other residents smiled every time they heard him – Timber, the bravest dog in the world. They would certainly sleep well tonight.

But Timber wasn't quite ready for sleep. He trotted around by himself one more time, glad to know that all the residents were happy and safe. He stopped to take a better look at the deep-red sky. Could it really be a warning? Had it something to do with Zora? He gave one last howl to the night and trotted back to the kennel. He was sure that the Grindlewood Army

would be called on again, but for now, all was well. The children and the residents were safe. The Wandeleis' magic was restored and Queen Wanda was in Hollow Hill planning their future. The WABOM was back where it belonged. So why did he feel so uneasy?

❧

Torn pages from *The Book of Darkness* lay on the floor of the bleak and draughty manor. They had provided enough magic to begin Zora's return from the Outer Oblivion, but it was going to take some time.

Lord Vargon sat in an armchair looking at Worfeus' wand on the table in front of him. There was no fire burning in the fireplace and no candles were lit around the room. It was cold, dark and eerie.

Suddenly, he banged his walking stick angrily on the thin, worn carpet. The buzzard shuddered and the augurer flinched.

'How could you make such a monstrous mess of things?' he cried. '*I* will be keeping this wand and *I* will present it to the mistress when she returns. There will be no more squabbling or messing up my plans. Is that understood?'

'Quite, my Lord Vargon,' muttered Audmund.

'Yes, my Lord,' said Bodric.

'I will devise a new plan to undo all your mistakes and lead us to our goal,' he said. 'In the meantime, prepare the potions, Audmund. Zora is going to need them. As for you, buzzard, tidy up that parchment and get out of my sight!'

The elderly tutor struggled out of his chair and slowly walked from the room, still muttering. He stopped and tilted his head, seeing his plan clearly in his own mind. 'Her revenge will begin in Grindlewood, where we will find the Wandeleis' source of power. She will be the most formidable leader any world has ever known, with me as her trusted advisor. Yes, the sorceress Zora will rule as she was meant to. Soon, she will make her triumphant return.'

THE END

Acknowledgements

I write alone in the peace and quiet of my writing room, which overlooks the Irish Sea. To produce each book, however, takes a lot of hard work by a very talented group of people.

A big thank you as always, to: my marvellous editor, Robert Doran, and my wonderful illustrator, Fintan Taite; to the mulit-talented Chenile Keogh for producing my book in all its forms; to Andrew Brown and Nigel Baker for their expert design work; to my extended family and close friends who continue to encourage and support my work; to my enthusiastic young readers, who I hope will enjoy this third outing; to all the booksellers, teachers and librarians everywhere who promote, facilitate and encourage reading every single day.

A special mention, also, for my amazing friend,

Peri Burnside and her beautiful Alaskan malamutes; and last, but never least, a huge thank you to my husband, Angelo, for all his help, encouragement, love and support.

Book 1

THE SECRETS OF GRINDLEWOOD

Jamie and Jemima Grindle move to Grindlewood House with their pets Timber and Teddy. But they soon realise that all is not as it seems in their beautiful new garden. There is dark magic at work in the nearby forest.

The good witch Wanda has been defeated and now the wicked warlock Worfeus is plotting to destroy Grindlewood and its enchanted garden. Only Wanda's powerful spells, written on a secret scroll, can rid the world of the warlock.

Timber must lead the animals of Grindlewood in their quest to find the scroll and defeat their enemy. But where is the scroll hidden and will they find it before Worfeus? Is there really enough magic in their wild garden to help them defeat such evil?

"A classic tale to delight readers aged 8-12."

Sue Leonard, Author and Journalist

Book 2

THE SECRET SCROLL

Grindlewood Book 2: The Secret Scroll follows the animals of Grindlewood garden as they continue the quest to save their enchanted home. The odds are stacked against them as they struggle to understand the ancient language of Wanda's secret scroll and use its magic to defeat the evil Worfeus.

Slowly Jamie and Jemima learn that their pets are caught up in something both sinister and special and that somehow they must find a way to help. All the while, the wicked warlock is growing more powerful and threatening.

The race is on to unlock the secrets of the scroll before Worfeus frees himself from the forest and enters the garden himself, intent on revenge and the destruction of Grindlewood.

Coming soon

BOOK 4 IN THE GRINDLEWOOD SERIES

ZORA'S REVENGE

While the sorceress Zora plans her revenge, the peace–loving Wandeleis find their magic is dangerously unstable. Unsure if they can match Zora's growing powers, they must prepare for a frightening encounter.

With another traitor in their midst and more of their treasures missing, it isn't long before the Wandeleis' magic is tested. They know their enemies are closing in fast, and their very existence is at stake.

Once again, Timber leads the Grindlewood Army as they try to save the Wandeleis from destruction. In their scariest quest so far, the children and their pets have their courage and loyalty tested to the limit. They must do everything they can to protect Grindlewood and guard the Wandeleis' precious secrets from Zora, but they no longer know who they can trust.

Available in autumn 2016